FEB.01.2005

D0866590

Hicks, Betty

Animal House and Iz

BETTY HICKS

ROARING BROOK PRESS
Brookfield, Connecticut

Hicks

For Lise, Sarah, Nate, and William,
who proved how much fun a blended family can have

ACKNOWLEDGMENTS

To Speck, Chessie, Frosty, Pollywacket, Bear, Iris, Gator, Tut, Superfish, Mork and Mindy, Tusker, Oreo, Chico, Pepi, Sailor, Dumbo, Patsy, Ginger, Red, Shadow, Satin, and all the many bugs, fish, frogs, turtles, crickets, praying mantises, snakes, salamanders, woolly worms, gerbils, chameleons, newts, and hermit crabs whose names I can no longer even remember.

Copyright © 2003 by Betty Hicks
Published by Roaring Brook Press
A Division of The Millbrook Press, 2 Old New Milford Road, Brookfield, Connecticut 06804
All rights reserved
Library of Congress Cataloging-in-Publication Data
Hicks, Betty.
Animal house & Iz / by Betty Hicks.
    p. cm.
Summary: Iz, formerly known as Elizabeth, has begun to enjoy the pandemonium of a spacey stepmother, mischievous stepbrothers, and an assortment of odd and unreliable pets.
[1. Stepfamilies—Fiction. 2. Family life—Fiction. 3. Pets—Fiction.] I. Title. II. Title: Animal house and Iz.
PZ7.H53155An 2003
    [Fic] —dc21   2002013356

ISBN   0-7613-1891-7 (trade)
            10 9 8 7 6 5 4 3 2 1
ISBN   0-7613-2746-0 (library binding)
            10 9 8 7 6 5 4 3 2 1

Book design by Jennifer Browne
Printed in the United States of America
First edition

Table of Contents

CaNNiBALs

"Iz!" Joey shouted. "They hatched!" He was going bananas. "Quick, Iz. You've got to see this!" I hadn't heard my stepbrother so excited since he discovered water balloons.

"See what?" I asked, glancing up from my book as he burst into my room. "What hatched?"

"My cocoon!" he yelled.

"No kidding." I pictured the spongy little blob he'd found attached to a broken branch. It had looked like a swirl of dirty foam, except it was crusty, and not much bigger than my thumb.

"Just let me finish this chapter," I said.

"No way," he shrieked, waving his hands. "You've got to come now!"

"Okay, okay." I closed *Shiloh* and tossed it onto my pillow. "This better be good."

I stood and stretched my arms. "So, what did you get?" I asked. "Butterflies? Moths?"

"No way." He grabbed my hand and started pulling me down the hall. "Come see. You won't believe it."

At first glance, Joey's room looked normal. Normal for Jack and Joey, that is. They're twins, and they share the same room, which, overall, smells like dead people. On any given day, it looks like a mad bomber blew up their closet. They look incredibly alike, except for Joey's hair, which is a shade blonder, and Jack's personality, which is a shade more like Rambo's.

Jack sat cross-legged on his wadded-up sheets, staring at something infinitesimal in the palm of his hand. *Infinitesimal* means teeny, as in unbelievably small. It's one of the words-of-the-day from the vocabulary calendar my mother gave me. Since I don't live with her anymore, I guess she wanted to make sure I stayed educated. Mostly, it's been a real nothing present, but once in a

2

while, I tear off a page and discover something cool.

I spotted movement across the room, and gaped at Joey's cocoon—the one we all learned later was not a cocoon. It was an egg sac. Hundreds of little white threads dangled from it. At the ends of the threads, tiny clear cases hung with wiggly things squirming in them.

"Joey," I gasped. "What is that?"

Then, right before my eyes, something tiny broke through one of the cases and climbed up over the swinging sacs and disappeared behind the branch. I leaned closer. The branch was crawling with things. Dozens and dozens of *infinitesimal* things. My skin crawled the way it would if an army of spiders was marching across my body.

"Look," said Jack, thrusting his open palm toward me.

"Isn't it awesome?" shouted Joey, jumping up and down.

I stared into Jack's hand. A *thing* stared back. There, perched in my stepbrother's grubby palm, was an impossibly small green face, shaped like a triangle, with bulging eyes and two super-long antennae. Its sticklike body had three pairs of legs, but the entire minibeast was no bigger than a mosquito. It held its front legs up in the air, folded.

"A praying mantis," I whispered in awe. "A perfectly formed, teeny, tiny, *infinitesimal* praying mantis."

"Yeah," said Joey. "See. It's praying."

"Yeah," said Jack. "Preying."

"Now I lay me down to sleep," Joey prayed.

"Attack!" Jack shouted.

"Dolt. You don't attack when you're praying."

"Sure you do. You hunt, then you pounce."

"What's hunting got to do with praying?" said Joey, waving his hands at Jack in frustration.

This was too funny.

"Uh, guys," I said, trying not to laugh. "It's a praying mantis, spelled p-r-a-y-i-n-g, because when it bends its front legs up in the air, it looks like it's saying a prayer."

About that time, a tiny praying mantis hiding in the folds of Jack's sheets sprang on one of its newly hatched brothers. And ate it.

4

"If you ask me," said Jack, grinning, "that mantis was p-r-e-y-i-n-g, which means he stalked his stupid brother, and turned him into lunch."

All of a sudden, I wondered if Jack might be right. How in the heck did you spell it? I stared at the little green monster, and thought, who cares? The insect crawling in Jack's bed is a cannibal.

Was that exciting or revolting? I didn't know. Part of me was totally grossed out, but most of me felt gleeful. Ever since Dad married Alice, and I inherited three crazy stepbrothers and a messy house, I'd been busy deciding between disgusting and cool.

Even my name was in doubt.

Mom calls me Elizabeth. Dad and Alice call me Liz. My stepbrothers call me Iz.

One part perfection, two parts casual, three parts crazy. That's my family.

So, who am I?

Alice says I'm whoever I want to be.

Mom says I'm her sunshine.

Dad says I ask myself too many questions.

At dinner that night, we were having hamburger-noodle casserole. Between bites, we told Dad and Alice about the praying/preying mantises. We had already shown them to Logan, my older step-brother. He wanted to build an experimental house for them all to live in.

A couple of years ago, I would have expected Alice to freak out over having a million carnivorous insects in one of her bedrooms. Now I knew better. Not only is she the mother of three pretty wacko sons, but she also teaches second grade. It takes a lot to upset her.

"Really!" Her eyes lit up. With her short, boyish haircut and her cute face, she looks a lot like Peter Pan.

"Yeah," said Joey proudly.

Joey, Jack, Logan, and I described them at the same time. Anyone who needs to master multiple conversations could learn a lot at our house.

After dinner, we all went straight to Jack and Joey's room.

"*Ta da!*" Joey flung open the door to his room.

Praying mantises were everywhere. On the curtains, the crumpled clothes on the floor, the box piled full of video games, the computer keyboard, a dog-eared and chocolate-stained copy of *Prince Caspian*, Joey's artist's easel, Jack's baseball trophies, the week-old pizza wedge with three curling pepperoni slices, and the rubber slab of fake vomit. There were even two mantises in Joey's turtle box, perched and praying (preying?) on top of Shellie, his pet turtle. The only place not covered in mantises was Jack's dry aquarium that housed Killer, his chameleon. I guess Killer had eaten his.

"Good grief," said Dad.

"Yikes," said Alice.

Yikes had to be the biggest reaction I'd heard from Alice in the entire two years she and Dad had been married. She pushed us back into the hall and slammed the door.

I knew exactly what Mom would've said. *Call pest control!*

"This calls for a party!" is what Alice said.

"A party?" we all asked, amazed.

"Yea!" shouted Joey. "A praying mantis party."

"Exactly," said Alice. "Call your friends. Invite them to the Great Praying Mantis Round-up. We've got to catch these things. I'll make root beer floats for everybody."

"Cool! Are we going to kill them?" Jack asked excitedly.

Sometimes I wonder about Jack.

"Not a chance," said Dad. He doesn't get psyched any easier than Alice does. "We'll put them in my garden. They'll eat every pest in sight."

"Will they eat Jack and Joey?" said Logan.

"Shut up," said Jack, pushing him. "Can I keep one?"

"Me, too," echoed Joey.

"I want twenty," said Logan. "To study." He's always studying weird things.

"Right." I laughed. "Pet praying mantises."

"Actually, Liz," Alice corrected me in a nice sort of way, "praying mantises make interesting pets. I'll tell you what. Promise to read about how

to look after them, and each of you can keep one."
She turned to Dad. "The rest go to work in the
garden."

The praying mantis party was wild. The slammed
door did not seal them in the bedroom. No, by the
time help arrived, they were all over the house.
Five of our friends tracked and bagged little green
monsters for over an hour. Sneaking. Trapping.
Pouncing. Laughing.

I may get confused about whether or not I
like cannibal insects, but I know I like the noise
and the fun. Every day, I feel less Elizabeth and
more Iz.

I should have called Claire, my best friend,
but I quit asking her over months ago. Whenever
Logan's around, she stops being regular Claire.
She becomes disgusting Claire, the coquette queen.
Coquette is a word-of-the-day that means a
female who flirts like an idiot and makes me want
to throw up.

Dad had more fun than anybody—pulling up

carpets, crawling around under furniture, and shouting, "Thar she blows!" Mom always said he looked half his age, like he was still in college. And acted that way, too. Me? I loved it, but I guess she didn't.

Was that why they didn't last—because Mom grew up and Dad didn't?

I was having too much fun to think about it.

Right after the Round-up, Jack, Joey, Logan, and I hatched our Get-a-Dog scheme. Mom, Dad, and Alice have major personality differences, but they do agree on one thing: No dogs. Actually, Dad's rule is no pets—except ones that can survive happily for three days, unattended. That means no dogs.

Every time they tell us that, we groan, "That's not fair."

And every time we complain, they smile and answer, "Life's not fair."

Jack, Joey, Logan, and I have major personality differences, too, but we definitely agree on one thing. Someday, some way, fair or not, we *will* have a dog.

You'd think casual Dad and Alice would love a dog. But, no. They'd rather be able to drop everything and take off on weekends, whenever the urge hits. They take us with them, but dogs need boarding, which means planning ahead.

Dad and Alice never plan ahead.

Talking my mother into owning a dog is not even thinkable. She's the perfection parent—the one who calls me Elizabeth. And perfection does not fit with chewed-on carpets and dog-doo. Besides, she's out of town a lot, which is why I live with Dad and Alice, three stepbrothers, and major chaos.

After the praying mantis party, Logan, Jack, Joey, and I collapsed in the den, scooping out the last of our root beer floats. Our friends had left, convinced that we had the coolest parents on earth.

It was Logan who hit on the idea for our Get-a-Dog plan. He's in the seventh grade, a year ahead of me, and three years older than the twins. But, if you ask me, he seems thirty years older than Jack and Joey.

"Look," he said. "We want a dog, right?"

"Right," we all answered, like some sort of chorus.

"Let's get a beagle," I said. I was reading *Shiloh*, and that's the stray dog Marty Preston, the boy in the book, had found. His parents didn't want him to have a dog, either, but at least they had a good reason. They couldn't afford to feed it.

"Nah," said Jack, "a Rottweiler."

"Scooby-Doo," added Joey.

It's not that we didn't have pets. Logan has Tiggy-the-hedgehog, Joey has Shellie-the-turtle, Jack has Killer-the-chameleon, and I have Glitz, a goldfish. And, now, we each have a baby praying mantis. But we all need something cuddly that comes when we call it.

"Mom thinks praying mantises are interesting," Logan explained. "You know, educational. I bet she and Rob would let us have more stuff like that."

Rob is my dad. It took me forever to get used to three boys calling him Rob instead of Mr. Becker. Even if he does act like a kid.

"So," I asked. "How does that get us a dog?"

"If we get enough weird animals and insects and stuff, and sort of, accidentally, lose control of them, they might decide that one measly dog would be easier." Logan crossed his arms and slouched back into the sofa cushion, clearly pleased with his idea.

"I want a tarantula!" shouted Jack.

"And an iguana!" added Joey.

"A python," said Jack, coiling his body and hissing dramatically.

"And a platypus," giggled Joey.

"Logan," I pointed out, rolling my eyes in serious doubt, "in case you haven't noticed, Alice and Dad never get freaked out."

Logan grinned, and slumped deeper into the couch. "Mom said *yikes* when she saw the praying mantises. She even slammed the door."

Jack, Joey, and I thought a minute. Alice had never slammed a door in her life. We smiled.

It might work.

BeCOMiNg FRoGs and FRiENds

The next day, Logan and I met each other in the middle-school library at lunchtime. We wanted to learn how to look after our praying mantises. We figured good research would impress Alice into letting us own more creatures. And, because Alice insisted on "real" books, not just the Internet. She might be laid back, but she was still a teacher.

Sifting through the J590s section (frogs, ants, alligators, snakes, bats, worms, spiders, sharks) reminded me of the last time Logan and I ended up in the animal zone of the library. It was a year ago, and Dad and Alice had taken us to a smooth, clear lake in the middle of the Blue Ridge Mountains.

Joey drew a great picture of the distant peaks with his blue crayon, because that's the color they look from far away. Alice explained that's how they got their name. I wanted to say, *"Duh!"* but I didn't. Alice is cool, but sometimes the teacher side of her gets carried away.

At the lake, we all changed into swimsuits and jumped in, splashing and kicking, and screaming, *brrrr!*

Away from the swimming area, Logan and I found the most amazing tadpoles in the shallow water. They were gigantic. As big as my fist.

I figured they would grow up to be bullfrogs. Logan guessed Texas toads. Jack and Joey thought they were the Monsters from the Black Lagoon.

"If they're Texas toads," I'd argued, "they're lost. This is North Carolina."

Logan had ignored me. Dad and Alice had been married a year, and that's how long Logan, Jack, and Joey had been ignoring me. You'd think *I* was the Monster from the Black Lagoon.

It's not that we fought when Dad and Alice got

married. No. We barely spoke. The first three months, all six of us tiptoed around each other like houseguests trying to win an Agreeable contest. Then, all that niceness, and the differences, got to be way too much. The truth was, we all irritated the fool out of each other.

They were so loud! Before Mom and Dad got divorced, I'd been used to my quiet-as-a-tombstone mom, and to being the only kid. After their divorce, I went to live with Dad, and, for a while, it got even quieter.

When it was just me and Dad, he had called me "the lady of the house," the one who noticed when the carpets needed to be vacuumed. Then he married Alice, and suddenly, *she* was in charge of that.

After a while, I stopped talking to anybody, except to argue about things like whose barbecued chicken was the best, Dad's or Alice's. Logan, Jack, and Joey goofed off, laughing themselves silly retelling childhood stories, pre-me, while I spent a lot of time in my room, e-mailing my misery to Claire.

Meanwhile, Dad and Alice took long walks after dinner. They'd leave the house, looking edgy and snapping at each other. Thirty minutes later they'd come back, holding hands and giving us kids pleading looks that said, *please like each other*.

But we didn't.

I was stuck, for the rest of my life, with enemy strangers. Then Logan and I found our tadpoles.

Dad and Alice went berserk with excitement, obviously because we'd done it together. They tried to make it look as though we'd made some great scientific discovery. Like finding fresh dinosaur eggs. They even agreed to let us bring three tadpoles home.

"For educational purposes," Alice said. But we knew it was a desperation move to give us something in common.

It worked.

We never did figure out what kind of frogs or toads they were, but we learned a lot of mindblowing things in the J590s section. For example, some toads can eat 86 flies in 10 minutes, and a

Southern Leopard frog named "Weird Harold" jumped 20 feet 3 inches!

Every day we watched our tadpoles swim around in the shallow water of our fish tank, but we still didn't say a whole lot to each other. Logan put in a rock that rose above the water so they could hop up when they became whatever it was they were going to turn into.

"Good idea," I told him.

Logan is actually very cool in his own, one-of-a-kind, sort of way. He wears red canvas high-top sneakers and Hawaiian-looking short-sleeved shirts, even in winter. The shirts all look like they came from a Good Will reject bin, but on him, they look good.

I added moss and leaves to the tank, to make it feel homier.

"Good idea," said Logan.

The tank sat on a shelf in Logan's room that looked like the lab where Frankenstein was born, filled with jars of oozy experiments. The rest of his room was crowded with miniature houses he'd designed out of cardboard scraps and Popsicle sticks. And his drum set.

"They need names," I suggested, pointing to the tadpoles.

"Yeah," he agreed. "But what?"

"Well." I lowered my finger, feeling silly. "There are three of them. We could name them after the three little pigs."

He scratched his head. "Did they have names?"

I felt dumb. I guess they didn't have names.

"Little pig, little pig," I said lamely.

He laughed. "How about Straw, Stick, and Brick?"

We both laughed.

I suggested the three wise men. I knew they all had names, but I couldn't come close to remembering one.

"Mal choir," I mangled.

"Balspar." He chuckled.

"How about the three musketeers?" he asked. "One of them was called D'art something with a tag sound in it."

"Dart tag. A frog named dart tag." I giggled.

"Fart tag." We both roared.

Eventually we settled on the Three Stooges—Larry, Curly, and Moe. Alice and Dad loved to rent their old black-and-white movies.

Slowly, the tadpoles grew back legs, one on each side of their tails. Then front legs. Their heads got thicker and their mouths wider. Their tails didn't fall off, like I thought they would. They just gradually got smaller and smaller until they weren't there anymore. It took two months, which meant they weren't bullfrogs, because they take longer than that. And they weren't lost Texas toads, because they didn't have enough warts.

Whatever they were, by the time we took Larry, Curly, and Moe back to their lake near Grandfather Mountain and released them, Logan and I had become friends, and I had become Iz. Jack and Joey liked Dad's barbecued chicken better than Alice's, and I liked Alice's better than Dad's. Joey drew me a perfect picture of Larry, Curly, and Moe to remember them by, and Jack asked me to come to his baseball games.

But the most amazing thing of all was that I loved our crazy, noisy house.

So, here we were in the J590s again. Dog books are in the J630s, far, far away. We were looking up the care and feeding of praying—*not* preying—mantises as pets. Believe it or not, there was actually a book about it. And believe it or not again, it said that the best insect pet of all was a praying mantis. Who knew? Besides Alice, that is.

It claimed they would eat from your hand. And come when you called! Unfortunately, it also mentioned they would try to *eat* your hand while they were sitting on it. Luckily, their mouths were too little to hurt.

Logan and I looked at each other and laughed. Jack and Joey were going to love their praying mantises.

"Hey, Logan. Hi, Iz."

It was Claire. All my friends call me Iz now. The hi in Hi, Iz was short and to the point. The *hey* in

21

Hey, Logan somehow had about twelve syllables in it.

"Hi," I muttered, snapping shut the praying mantis book and heading for the checkout desk before I barfed.

When we got home from school, we all went straight to our rooms to check on our praying mantises, and to see if they needed more pieces of leftover hamburger casserole.

Joey had surfed the net last night until he found information on feeding them. That was fine with Alice, since it was the best we could do on short notice.

He learned that babies will eat tiny bits of meat. For now. But once they're adults, they'll eat only food that's still alive and kicking. *Erk.*

Jack, of course, was used to that. He'd been feeding Killer, his chameleon, big, fat flies and cheerfully sacrificing gross, wiggly mealworms to him for months. He kept the mealworms in the refrigerator in a store-bought plastic container filled with dry oatmeal-looking stuff. The flies he caught himself. A pretty creepy talent, but still— not something just anybody can do.

My mantis was in a shoebox I'd covered with a piece of screen. He perched on a stick, front legs raised, eyeing me. He seemed to be saying, *Got any steak?*

"Iz!" shouted Jack over the sound of Logan playing his drums. "Telephone."

I glanced through Logan's open door on my way to the phone. He was pounding away, head jerking, hair flopping, unaware of anything but rhythm.

I know zero about music, but I thought he sounded pretty good.

I picked up the hall phone. It was Mom, unexpectedly home for two days. Something about dinner.

"Mom," I said. "Talk louder. Logan's playing his drums."

"Elizabeth, sweetheart," she repeated. "Can you come to dinner tonight and spend the night?"

"Oh, Mom . . . I don't know." I hesitated. Sure, I wanted to see her, but not tonight. We were fixing up permanent homes for our praying mantises tonight. And deciding what new pets we all wanted—the important first step in the Get-a-Dog plot.

"I can't tonight, Mom," I answered.

"Oh." She sounded disappointed. "How about tomorrow, then?"

Tomorrow was when Logan, Jack, Joey, and I planned to ask for the first round of our pet parade.

"I'm sorry, Mom. I can't come tomorrow, either."

Silence on her end of the phone.

"I've got a project I'm working on," I continued. "And I've got to be here to do it. All the stuff's here." That wasn't exactly a lie.

"Well," she said sadly, "okay."

A wave of guilt washed over me.

"So," she said in a fake cheerful voice. "Tell me what you've been doing."

I told her all about the Great Praying Mantis

24

Hatching. I didn't mention the Round-up, or the root beer floats.

"Good grief," she said. "I hope you called pest control."

"Yeah," I said. That wasn't totally a lie either. She didn't say pest control had to be professional.

"When will you be back in town?" I asked.

"I'm on a new job. In London. It could be three weeks or more."

Mom is some kind of efficiency expert. She goes all over the world, fixing people's businesses. Big corporations practically wait in line for her, she's so good.

Three weeks, I thought. Major guilt stabbed me in the chest. All for a praying mantis . . . and what could turn out to be a very iffy shot at getting a dog.

"Mom," I said. "Maybe I can come tonight. I'll work something out. Okay?"

"Oh! Sweetheart, that would be wonderful! And I have a surprise for you." I felt sunshine beaming through the phone.

I hung up. Spending twenty-four hours away

from my house, there was no telling what could happen. Jack could hatch a dragon. Logan might discover kryptonite. Alice could plan a picnic to Mars.

Crash! The sound of slamming and banging reached me, even over the thumping of Logan's drums. It came from Jack and Joey's room.

"That's *my* praying mantis!"

"It is not! It's mine!"

"Stupid! Mine ate yours."

"*You're* stupid. That one's mine!"

"It is not!"

"Is, too!"

Blam!

I loved my mother, but I hated missing out.

IZ WHIZ

7:00. Mom and I sat down to eat dinner in her deluxe townhouse. Oriental rugs, a complete leather-bound collection of Shakespeare with raised gold lettering that I loved to run my fingers across, incredible orchid collection, fine china, filet mignon with a reduced Burgundy sauce, and asparagus with toasted almonds. She's a great cook.

She's also beautiful. More than beautiful, she's elegant. You'd never guess we were related. Her long brown hair shines like the mahogany dining room table that my elbows were propped on. She wears it pulled back in one long, perfect braid, every hair in place.

My hair is boring brown, like a mouse, and

insanely curly. I pull it back in a ponytail. Even so, half the pieces escape the rubber band and frizz around my face. The other half wouldn't braid for a million dollars.

As I took a bite of the tender, scrumptious steak, I wondered if Nelson (that's what I named my praying mantis) would eat meat with wine on it. Would it make him drunk?

"How's life at your dad's house?" asked Mom.

"Great!" I practically shouted, then wished I hadn't sounded so excited. If we'd been eating salmon instead of steak, the expression on Mom's face would have meant that she'd just swallowed a fish bone.

"And the dot-com business?" she asked sarcastically.

Dad's a freelance commercial artist, but a year ago, he started an extra business on the Internet—selling trips to last-minute travelers like he and Alice were. It failed. Mom knew that.

The last time we talked about it, she gave me a lecture on needing to have your marketing money in sync with something. She used a lot of words like *collateral* and *viable* and *analysis*. I didn't understand a word she said.

Where was the mom who had laughed at my knock-knock jokes and read me fairy tales aloud, acting out the wicked witch parts while I giggled? When, I wondered, had Mom gotten so super serious? And so boring? And why?

"He's got a ton of art jobs right now," I answered. "Real busy."

Mom carefully cut one asparagus spear into four perfect bites. "Elizabeth," she said. "I've missed you."

"Me, too, Mom." I meant it. I did miss her. Especially the mom I remembered, the happier one who hadn't been gone all the time. But I missed the bigger Becker household even more. The noise, my messy room, even the dirty dishes that were always piled in the kitchen sink.

It was the new me.

"Uh, Mom." I didn't know how to bring this up, but I loved my new name, too. On the way over here in the car tonight, I'd asked Dad to start calling me Iz.

"Instead of Liz?" he'd asked, surprised.

"Yeah."

He thought a minute.

I wondered if he was remembering how he sometimes called me his Little Liz Whiz.

"You really like Iz?" he asked.

"Yes, Dad." I looked straight at him. "I do. It's me now. Don't you think?"

"Well." He reached across the gearshift and patted my knee. "I guess it is."

"And Alice will call me that, too?"

"You'll have to ask her, but no problem. I know she'll be fine with it."

"Thanks, Dad."

"Happy to oblige, Iz."

As we pulled into the parking lot of Mom's townhouse, I realized that Dad seemed far away, as if something was bugging him. I wondered if he was noticing her new Lexus next to his old Ford minivan. It wasn't like Dad to care about cars. So, why did he seem worried all of a sudden?

"Uh, Iz," he said.

"Yeah, Dad?"

"Does this mean I can't call you my Little Liz Whiz anymore?"

I laughed, then leaned across the seat and kissed him on the cheek. "How about your Little Iz Whiz, Dad?"

He slapped the steering wheel. "Hey!" he exclaimed, grinning. "I think I like that even better."

Now, here I was with Mom. What would she say?

"Uh, Mom. Did you know that my friends call me Iz now?"

"What?" she said.

"Iz," I answered.

"Oh," she laughed. "Kids come up with the craziest things."

"No, Mom. It's really my name now. And I like it. Logan and Jack and Joey call me that. And Dad and Alice." Well, I thought, not Alice yet, but I knew she would.

"And, Mom . . . I want you to, too."

"Is?" she asked, in a foggy voice.

31

"Yeah," I repeated. "Iz."

Mom looked majorly challenged. Like someone trying to grasp Chinese.

"*Is* is not a name," she said. "It's a verb."

"What?" I didn't get it.

"A verb," she repeated. "*Is* is a verb."

"Oh," I laughed. "It's not *I-s*. It's *I-z*. You know, Liz without the *L*. Iz."

"*Iz?*" She looked stunned. "But, sweetheart. You have a beautiful name. Elizabeth Ellington Becker. You want me to call you *Iz?*"

"Yep," I said, trying to sound confident. "Iz Becker. That's me." I smiled.

Mom circled her fork around and around in her reduction sauce, making little rivers of it all over her Herend china plate.

"Okay," she said finally. "If you're sure."

For a long time, neither of us said a word.

She sighed a couple of times and gazed off into space. Probably picturing Elizabeth Ellington Becker, the beautiful, promising newborn baby who, eleven years later, turned into a verb.

"Eliz—I mean, Iz," she said eventually. Her face brightened. "What was the vocabulary word on your calendar today?"

I couldn't remember. Actually, I was at least a week behind tearing off the days. What was a word from last week? Come on, Iz. Think of something. Don't hurt her feelings again.

"*Metamorphosis*," I blurted. It wasn't really a word-of-the-day. It was what I'd been tested on in science yesterday, but it was the only big word I could think of.

Mom's face relaxed into a smile.

I proudly quoted what I'd memorized from my science book. "It's 'a profound change in form from one stage to the next in the life history of an organism.' Like tadpoles to frogs," I said. "Or caterpillars to butterflies," I added, trying to spear the last piece of asparagus on my plate.

"Or Elizabeth to Iz," said Mom.

I jerked my head up. She was grinning. The mom I remembered. We both laughed.

"About my surprise," she said, standing up to

clear the dishes. "How would you like a pet that stayed at my house?"

I couldn't believe what I was hearing.

"A dog!" I screeched. "You're getting a dog?"

"No," she said gently. "Go look in your room."

I flew up the stairs. There, on top of my bookcase, was an aquarium, complete with pumps and fancy filters. Swimming around it in were five of the most awesome tropical fish I'd ever seen. Bright blues, greens, and yellows. They made Glitz, my goldfish at Dad's house, look like a sick guppy.

I didn't know what to think. My mom was going to keep an aquarium? I knew what a smelly mess it was to clean my tiny goldfish bowl. I gagged every time I did it. She would do that for me?

"What do you think?" she said, entering the room behind me.

I turned and gave her a hug. "They're beautiful," was all I could say. "Who's going to clean the tank?" I asked. Okay, that wasn't the second thing that should have come out of my mouth, but it did.

"Well," she said, slipping one arm around my shoulders, "I'd love for you to spend more time with me, and we could do it together."

When I didn't answer, she gave me an extra squeeze and added, "But I'll clean it when you're not here."

"But who's going to feed them when you're not here?" My brain was still trying to understand what Mom-buying-complicated-fish meant.

"The lady who comes by to water my orchids," she answered.

"Oh." I stared at my fish. They were gorgeous. Graceful and elegant. Like my mother. So why wasn't I more thrilled?

And why did Mom keep looking at me, hopefully, like I should be more excited?

And why did I keep asking myself questions?

WORmS FOR DiNNeR

Nelson had grown. Honest. By the time I got home from school after spending the night at my mother's, my praying mantis was bigger. And hungrier.

Logan had left him in the temporary box I'd put together. He and Jack and Joey had decided not to fix up new homes for them after all. The book claimed you could leave them out, like on a curtain or something, and they'd pretty much stay there, waiting for their next meal to walk by.

I took Nelson out of his shoebox and placed him on my window curtain. Not convinced that a five-course meal would stroll past him, I went to the kitchen and rummaged around in the fridge until I found a pack of bologna. I took a piece back to my room.

Watching Nelson eat was amazing.

After he pounced on the food and gobbled it up, he cleaned himself. He washed his face with his front legs, then wiped his eyes with them. He even slid them through his mouth. I stared open-mouthed, watching all the grooming movements of a cat being made by a tiny six-legged green insect with bulging bug eyes.

Down the hall, Logan was pounding away on his drums again. Fortunately, Tiggy sleeps in the basement. That's short for "Mrs. Tiggy-winkle." Logan named him Spike until *he* turned out to be a *she*. Then he renamed her for the hedgehog in the *Peter Rabbit* books.

Logan may seem like a wild musician and mad inventor to his friends, but I know better. Deep down he's a marshmallow. Soft. Sweet. It would not surprise me if he could name every single character in all twenty-three *Peter Rabbit* books.

Tiggy sleeps all day, because that's what hedgehogs do. And they need calm, quiet places to snuggle into. Logan's room is not a calm, quiet place.

So she spends her days burrowed into a hole in the back of a sofa cushion in the basement. She wakes up around dinnertime and scratches on the bottom step until Logan carries her up to his room. He built an ultracool, very complicated house for her there, filled with mazes and hide-boxes. From sunset to sunrise, she runs around as hyper as Jack and Joey after hot fudge sundaes and Coke.

Logan sleeps through it.

Zoweee! Nelson, on my windowsill, wasn't praying. Clearly, he was preying. Frozen in place, watching a tiny spider crawl closer and closer. Suddenly Nelson's front legs shot out faster than light and seized the guy. *Crunch. Gulp.* Gone.

I decided to take Nelson outdoors for a bite.

Joey came flying past me, holding his hand over his mouth.

"Uhm g'nuh wurf!"

Slam! He disappeared into the bathroom.

I'm guessing he said, *I'm gonna barf!*

Jack came strolling down the hall, laughing.

"What's the matter with Joey?" I asked.

"He cooked some oatmeal," he answered innocently.

"And?" I knew there had to be more.

"He ate it."

"And?"

"It had my mealworms in it."

"Oh, gag." Maybe we already had enough creatures to launch our Get-a-Dog plot.

We all sat down to dinner. At Mom's house, we ate at 7:00. Always. But the dinner hour for Dad and Alice was all over the place. Mostly they just tried to make sure we ate together.

Part One of the GAD plan (short for Get-a-Dog) was to ask for new pets—gradually. Logan wanted to call it the GLAD plan, as in, Get Logan a Dog, but we overruled him. Even though GLAD did sound better.

Logan was going first and asking for a ferret. They're so wired, they'd make Tiggy-the-hyper-hedgehog look like a slug.

Joey still looked a little green from throwing up mealworms, but we agreed this wasn't the right time to tell Dad and Alice about his after-school snack.

"You look green," said Dad.

"I'm okay," Joey muttered.

"You're sure?" asked Alice.

"Yeah."

Alice scooped up a spoonful of macaroni and plopped it on Joey's plate, next to his pork chop. Joey stared at it. He turned from green to chalk.

"Worms!" he exclaimed. "That looks like worms."

"Don't be goofy," said Alice.

"Easy for you to say," said Joey. He faked a gag. At least, I think it was faked.

"What's that supposed to mean?" asked Dad, coming to the defense of Alice's cooking.

"It means *your* brother didn't try to poison *you*," Joey blurted.

Uh-oh. Part One of our plan was about to go off-course.

"I did not poison you!" shouted Jack.

"You did."

"I did not."

Logan and I kicked them both under the table, but it was too late. They were on a roll. Dad and Alice were whipping their heads back and forth, like they were watching ping-pong.

"Oh, yeah?" said Joey. "Then who put mealworms in my cereal bowl and left it on the kitchen counter—covered with oatmeal—looking like all it needed was water and a microwave?"

"You are so stupid," said Jack. "I dumped my worms and meal in a bowl to see how many were left."

"Liar."

"Idiot."

"Am not."

"What did you think they were?" said Jack. "Dancing raisins?"

"Enough," said Dad.

"Joey," said Alice. "Did you eat mealworms today?"

"Yeah." Joey looked down at his plate, embarrassed.

"Did you throw them all up?"

"Yeah."

"Then I think you'll be fine," she said, dropping a spoonful of macaroni onto my plate. She sneaked me a quick smile that said, *aren't boys a riot?*

"They're a good source of protein," said Dad. His face was serious, but his eyes were laughing.

Logan and I immediately launched into damage control. We told them all the fascinating things we'd learned about our praying mantises.

"They are soooo interesting," I said. "I can't wait to read more insect books."

"Yeah," said Logan. "I may check them all out."

"Great," said Alice. "Would you like me to drive you to the library downtown?"

"No!" we blurted. "But thanks."

Dad and Alice chatted about his new job for a while. He's been hired to do all the artwork for a huge ad campaign.

Eventually, Logan noticed a lull, and asked for a ferret.

"A ferret?" said Alice.

"And an iguana!" shouted Joey, unable to stop himself.

"And a tarantula," said Jack.

Logan and I threw dagger looks at both of them. Part One of GAD had just jumped the tracks again.

"Okay," said Alice.

"Really?" we all exclaimed.

"Sure." She put down her fork and smiled at Dad, who was watching her like she'd been out in the sun too long.

"With a few restrictions, of course."

Of course, I thought, my bubble bursting. Joey and Jack were still panting like eager puppies, though.

"All of those things can be fed food and water that'll last longer than three days," said Logan, sounding knowledgeable.

We'd been expecting the three-day rule, so we'd already read up on the care of about a million creatures. But Alice had said *restrictions*, with an *s*. What else?

"You have to look after them yourselves—"

"No problem!" we shouted. I began to feel hopeful again.

"I mean *really* look after them," she said. "That means you read everything there is to know. How long they live, what they eat, why they make good pets, and why they don't. So you can't mistreat them, or misunderstand them, not even accidentally." She paused and looked us each in the eye. "Understood?"

"Understood," we repeated in chorus.

I was getting excited again. I had decided I wanted a sugar glider. It's like a flying squirrel, but even cuter, with big eyes.

"And," said Alice, "you have to pay for everything yourselves. The animal, the cage, food, vet bills, everything."

Dad smiled and relaxed into his chair. Logan, Jack, Joey, and I slumped. Good-bye, sugar glider. Good-bye, ferret. Good-bye, GAD.

Sugar gliders and ferrets cost at least a hundred dollars. Iguanas and tarantulas, who knows? More than Jack and Joey had, that was for sure. I was secretly relieved about the tarantula, though. The thought of Jack-the-wanna-be-Ripper with one was scarier than Dracula's coffin.

"Can I ask for a ferret for my birthday?" asked Logan.

"Afraid not." Alice shook her head and smiled sympathetically.

"That's not fair," grumbled Jack.

"Life's not fair," said Dad, grinning.

"I want you to pay for it yourself," Alice continued. "You'll value it more."

Now what? I wondered. We could make our own cages and pay for food out of our allowances, but what animals were free? Sometimes kittens were free, but they definitely had vet bills. Big ones. Besides, Jack and Dad didn't like cats.

"Can I have a cockroach?" asked Jack.

"No!" Five voices shouted at once.

"Let's drive to the beach tomorrow," said Dad, out of nowhere.

"Yes!" exclaimed Alice. "I love the beach in

April. Short-sleeve shirts. The sun on my arms. The first warm days of spring." She hugged herself.

Done. Decided.

Logan, Jack, Joey, and I looked helplessly at each other. Defeated.

Do HEDGeHOGs EAt SNaKEs?

Claire grabbed me in front of my locker on Monday and wanted to know everything about our beach trip. *Everything* meant she wanted to know what Logan did, what he said, what he wore, what he ate, and how many breaths he took.

She was driving me insane. I missed regular Claire, my used-to-be best friend.

I tried to tell her about our trip. "We drove to Wrightsville Beach," I said.

"Did you sit next to Logan?" she asked.

"Jack, Joey, Logan, and I played road rage all the way there in the car," I answered. "It was so funny. We made up dopey driver insults, and Dad and Alice gave us points, from one to ten, for the best ones."

"Did Logan win?" asked Claire.

I ignored her and said, "I got five points for, 'You're going to love driving as soon as you learn how.' I thought it should have been worth eight, though."

"How many points did Logan get?"

"Joey got nine for 'Hey! Let us lead, you under-speed centipede,'" I answered.

"What did Logan make up?"

"Jack," I answered, "*lost* twenty points for saying, 'Let us pass, you stupid ass.'"

Claire laughed.

Finally . . . the old Claire.

"Your parents are so cool," she said. "Mine would have lectured all the way there that road rage is 'unacceptable behavior.'"

"Yeah." I laughed. "I don't know why Dad and Alice let us do it. They're the last two people on the planet to rant or rage about anything."

"Maybe they're using reverse psychology. You know, letting you blow off steam so that you'll actually be calm."

"Maybe," I said, but I doubted it. Claire thinks she's a psychiatrist. But I think Dad and Alice were probably just letting us be creative, and not bored, on the way to the beach. They're big into creative.

"I'll bet it will keep Jack from becoming a psychopath," said Claire.

Where did she get this stuff?

"Jack brought back a hermit crab," I said.

"Did Logan find one?" asked Claire, twisting a piece of her long, blond hair around her finger.

"Will you *please* let it rest about Logan!" I screamed.

The color drained from Claire's face. She was speechless, but only for a second. "What's the matter with you!" she shouted back. "You have been so rude for months, and weird, and stuck-up . . . and . . . and . . . I don't know what else. You're a pain in the butt!" she exclaimed.

She wheeled around and stomped off down the hall. Half the sixth grade stared after her, then looked at me. I wanted to shout after her, *You're going to love being a best friend as soon as you learn how.* I kicked my locker and headed for social studies.

When I got home from school, I flopped down on my bed and stared at Glitz. "I wish you were a dog," I groaned.

Glitz swam back and forth, opening his mouth, closing his mouth. That's about all goldfish do. I thought about my tropical fish at Mom's house, and how she wanted to spend more time with me. I thought about my blowup with Claire.

I needed to hug a dog. Right now. Here I was in a house full of animals, and not one was huggable—unless Jack, Joey, or Logan counted. I looked at Nelson, locked onto my window curtain, his green swivel head scanning the territory for groceries. The thought of hugging a praying mantis should have made me giggle, but I was too depressed.

I thought about waking Tiggy up. Not that I could hug a breathing pincushion, but I did love holding her. She always nestled into my lap and

50

made soft purring sounds. If adorableness were rated on a scale of one to ten, hedgehogs would be a twelve. And they actually do curl up into balls like the ones the queen played croquet with in *Alice in Wonderland*.

I knew better than to wake her up, though. Disturbed hedgehogs make a noise that shatters glass.

"*Ta da!*" exclaimed Joey, bounding into my room and holding out his screen-covered bug box. Inside was a cricket.

"Meet Chester. I caught him at school today. He's named after *The Cricket in Times Square*."

"And I found a garter snake," said Logan, following him into my room and proudly presenting a small, striped, twisting reptile for my approval.

"Wow! Can I hold him?" I'm not a big snake lover, but this little guy was almost cute.

The snake coiled itself around my fingers. It felt like a live rubber rope hugging my hand. I'd still rather hug a dog, though.

"GAD, Part Two," announced Logan, flinging his arms up in victory.

"Do you think we have enough?" I asked.

"Yeah," said Joey. "We have four praying mantises." He held up four dirty fingers.

Jack and Joey had settled their which-mantis-ate-whose dispute by recapturing one Dad had released into the garden. They kept them in separate containers now.

"And one turtle." Joey held up another filthy finger. "A goldfish, a chameleon, a hedgehog, a hermit crab, a garter snake, and a cricket." Joey ran out of fingers before he could count his cricket. He stared at his hands, disappointed that he didn't have one more finger to prove his point with.

"Anyway," he said, dropping his fingers, "that's eleven. And as soon as you find something, we'll have twelve!"

What could I find? Nelson ate everything that creeped or crawled. Besides, I didn't want anything else that creeped or crawled . . . or swam. I wanted a dog.

"I found the snake in Dad's garden," said Logan.

"Maybe we can find another one for you."

"No, thanks." I handed him back his snake. "It might eat Nelson." I was amazed at how much I liked Nelson. I loved the way he cocked his head and listened when I talked.

"You got any money?" said Joey. "Maybe you could buy a hamster."

I shook my head. "Even if I could afford one, they need expensive cages and stuff.

"Look," I said. "Let's forget about me. I'll think of something. What can we do with what we've already got?"

Logan stared at his snake as it slithered around his arm.

Chir-rip! Chir-rip! chirped Chester.

"Man, that is one loud cricket," said Logan.

"That's it!" I exclaimed. "We can put Chester in Dad and Alice's bedroom before they go to sleep. He'll keep them awake all night."

"And Tiggy, too," said Joey. "That hedgehog could keep Rip Van Winkle awake, scratching and scrambling, and running all over the place."

"Great idea," said Logan. "But we'd better let Tiggy and Chester loose on different nights. I think hedgehogs eat crickets."

"Oh," said Joey and I together.

Joey brightened. "We could put your snake in their bed!"

"Do hedgehogs eat snakes?" Logan wondered out loud. "Would snakes eat crickets?"

Was he seriously considering the snake-in-the-bed idea?

"Look," I said. "We'd better make a list of who eats who . . . or whom." I never could remember which word was right.

Shoot, I thought, the Elizabeth side of me was the one that tried to remember things like when to use *whom*. I'm Iz now. Iz might even go for the snake-in-the-bed idea.

I grinned. "If we turn everything loose at once, we could end up with no pets at all. Well, only one big fat one with serious indigestion."

Joey and Logan laughed.

"Iz," shouted Jack from downstairs. He must

have just gotten back from baseball practice. "Telephone."

Heck, I thought. I hated to leave the plot planning. And only a few minutes ago, I'd been depressed. I smiled and hurried down the hall to the phone. Maybe it would be the old Claire, calling to apologize for the new Claire.

It was Mom, calling from London.

"Sweetheart," she said. The connection was so clear, you'd think she was calling from next door. "How's my sunshine?" She sounded really happy.

"Great, Mom. What's up?"

"My job's going faster than anyone thought," she said. "I'll be home next week."

"That's cool." A part of me really did think it was cool, but another part of me didn't want to stay with her next week. GAD, Part Two, would be in full swing by then.

"And Eliz—I mean, Iz. I've got some really exciting plans to talk to you about."

"What?" I asked. Maybe she was moving to

London or Paris or somewhere to be closer to her work. Would that be bad or good?

"I miss you," she said, suddenly sounding sad and serious. "I'm going to quit traveling and work in town. I've thought about it, and I can do consulting. Smaller jobs, less money, but"—I could hear the excitement building in her voice—"life's not about money, is it?"

"Uh, no, Mom. Of course not." She was going to live here in town. Permanently. What did that mean?

"Don't you see what that means, Elizabeth? It means you can live with me now."

PET THReATS

After Mom dropped her news bomb, I slogged back to my room. My face felt like it does when I have a fever, so I knew I probably had big red blotches all over it. It does that when I get uptight. And my brain was spinning.

I knew I didn't want to live with my mother, but I couldn't tell her that . . . could I? Today, I'd told Claire how I felt. Look where that got me.

I wished Claire were here now. She had her faults, but she was great at figuring stuff out, back when she used to be a good listener.

Okay, Iz, I thought. *You* figure it out.

Claire hates me. That's bad. Part Two of GAD is looking up. That's good. Everybody's found an

extra pet but me. That's bad again. Mom loves me
too much. Was that bad or good?

I didn't know . . . but I knew I didn't want to
live with her.

Jack, Joey, and Logan were all in my room, looking up which animals eat each other. All the books
Logan and I had checked out were spread out on
the floor, opened. My room's the only one *with* a
floor. Jack's hermit crab was inching its way side-
ways across my unmade bed.

"He better not poop on my sheets," I said.

"Hey, Iz," said Logan, not looking up. "Look
what we found." He pointed to a picture that
looked just like Joey's turtle. "Shellie eats grass
and dandelions."

"Huh?" said Joey. "I've been giving her dog
food and raw hamburger."

"That's okay," said Logan. "She eats that, too.
And insects. I guess that makes her a pet threat to
Chester and the mantises."

"Whoa," said Jack, looking up from a book with

a cobra on the front. "Put Hiss Majesty at the top of the list."

"*Hiss Majesty?*" I blurted.

"Yeah," said Logan, still flipping through his turtle book. "That's what I named my garter snake. I'm calling him Hiss, for short." He glanced up at me.

"What happened to you?!" he exclaimed, staring at my face.

"Nothing," I muttered, trying to wish away the splotches. I didn't want to get into this whole thing about Mom right now. Maybe later.

"Do you guys want to hear what snakes eat or not?" said Jack, irritably.

"Yes!" I exclaimed, too loud.

Logan eyed me suspiciously.

"They eat frogs, toads, tadpoles, salamanders, worms, leeches, small mammals, birds—"

"What kind of small mammals?" asked Logan. "Would Hiss eat a hedgehog?"

Jack flipped ahead a couple of pages. "It doesn't say anything about hedgehogs. But here's an awesome picture of a little snake swallowing a really big rat!"

"Tiggy's way too big to swallow," I said, looking at Logan's garter snake and trying to imagine it gulping down something the size of a softball.

"Maybe," said Jack, "but look at this." He held up the picture of the snake with something huge and furry stuffed in his mouth. "It says here they unhitch their jaw and drag things three times wider than their heads down their throats."

I rummaged around the mess on top of my desk and grabbed a pencil and a piece of paper. "I'll make a chart of what you find."

I drew a few lines up and down, and a bunch across, then started filling in the blank spaces. I put Turtle in the first box. Then I wrote Shellie's name and what she ate.

Next came Hiss.

I stopped writing. "Do snakes eat fish?"

"Hold on." Jack flipped back through the pages again. "Yeah." He grinned. "They especially like the entrails."

"What are entrails?" asked Joey.

"Guts," Jack answered gleefully.

I stuck my tongue out and twisted my face into a yucky shape. Then I added Glitz to Hiss's dinner list.

Jack, Joey, and Logan looked up pet diets. I wrote it all down.

When I got to Jack's hermit crab, I got confused.

"It says here," said Logan, pointing his finger at his open book, "that he'll eat anything, but it's best to feed him oats, vegetables, and fruit with a little peanut butter."

He moved his finger to the next page. "That's because he buries his uneaten food in the sand, so unless you want your room to smell like rotting flesh, don't give him meat."

"Let's give him meat," said Jack, grinning.

"Your room already smells like rotting flesh," said Logan.

"He'd eat Glitz," I said, trying not to imagine the reek of dead goldfish, buried for a week.

"And Chester, too," added Joey.

We all looked at the tiny seashell, no bigger than a walnut, that was still creeping across my bed. A bunch of red legs stuck out and propelled it along. One big pincer claw led the way. Except for the claw, Captain Hook, in his seashell home, looked harmless.

"I don't think he'd mess with Glitz or Chester unless they were already dead," said Logan, as he slowly turned the pages of his book, looking for more clues. "It doesn't sound like he'd actually kill anybody."

"So, what do I put?"

"That Captain Hook is a lean, mean eating machine," said Jack.

I stuck my tongue out at Jack and wrote: "Hermit Crab. Captain Hook. Eats (but won't kill) everybody—probably."

"Done," I declared, putting down the pencil and paper. "Now we know which animals are safe together and which aren't."

I saw the edge of my word calendar peeking

out from under the empty Cheese Doodles package on my desk. I reached over and pushed the package aside. The top page read: "*Prudence: wise thought before acting; good judgment.*"

"See?" I ripped it off and held it out for everyone to read. "A perfect omen for GAD."

I tossed it aside and pinned the Who Eats What list onto my cluttered corkboard, being careful not to cover up Joey's frog drawing. "When we plan each step of our attack," I said proudly, "we look at this first. That's *prudence!*"

Logan groaned. "Come on, Iz. A vocabulary calendar?"

"How lame can you get?" said Jack.

"That is so dumb," said Joey.

My face flushed hot. "A little knowledge wouldn't exactly kill you guys, you know."

Oh, my gosh! I sounded like my mother.

"Cool chart, though," said Logan, pretending he hadn't just slammed me.

"Idiots," I muttered.

Joey looked kind of sorry, but didn't know how

to say it, so he timidly picked up Captain Hook and held him in his hand. *Fwoop!* The red legs disappeared up into the shell so fast, you'd think Joey had pushed the tiny crab's *retract* button.

"So," I said. "What should we do first?"

"Operation Cricket," said Joey, tossing Captain Hook to Jack.

"Hey," shouted Jack. "Don't throw him!"

"Sorry."

"*Yow!*" Jack yelped. "He bit me!"

We all stared at Jack's hand. A small red claw stuck out from a seashell and pinched Jack's palm. At first it hung on, dangling, as Jack cried, "Leggo! Leggo! Leggo!" frantically shaking his hand back and forth.

Then Captain Hook went flying through the air and landed, *plop*, on my pillow.

"You did that on purpose!" Jack screamed.

"No," said Joey, looking pale. "I didn't. Honest."

"You did, too."

"I did not!" Joey turned from sorry to mad.

"Quiet," said Logan. "Both of you. Joey didn't mean to. Okay?"

Jack stared at the bright red mark on his hand. It was already beginning to swell.

"Yeah, maybe," he muttered.

"Now," asked Logan, "where were we? Oh, yeah . . . Joey. Operation Cricket."

"Yeah!" Joey brightened. "Tonight, I'll put Chester in Mom and Rob's room. He'll chirp all night."

"Perfect," said Logan. "Tomorrow, Tiggy can keep them awake."

"The next night we can put Captain Hook in their bed," said Jack rubbing his sore hand. The thought made him stop wincing and smile wickedly.

"Then comes the snake," he hissed. "*Sssss.*"

friends 4ever

Logan stumbled out of my room carrying all the library books. Jack marched out, holding Captain Hook in his left hand and sucking the wound on his right one. Joey hung around, watching Nelson scope the world from my window curtain.

"I wish I could leave my praying mantis out," he said. "But even if Jack's mantis didn't eat him, Killer or Shellie would."

He ambled over and read my "Who Eats What" chart.

WHO EATS ~~WHO/WHOM~~ WHAT

Animal	Name	Eats	Comments
Turtle	Shellie	insects, fruit, vegetation, dog food	mostly vegetarian but might eat Chester or Nelson
Snake	Hiss	insects, rodents, frogs, slugs, worms, fish	will eat Chester, Nelson, and Killer. Tiggy? Glitz
Goldfish	Glitz	fish food	won't eat anybody
Praying Mantis	Nelson	insects, meat	would eat everybody if it could. But it can't. (we think)
Cricket	Chester	bread, fruit, plants, insects, spiders	could eat Nelson
Hedgehog	Tiggy	spiders, insects, snails, worms, slugs, cat food	will eat Nelson and Chester
Chameleon	Killer	crickets, mealworms, spiders, flies	will eat Chester, Nelson, and Joey
Hermit Crab	Captain Hook	anything (oats, veggies, fruit, and peanut butter best)	eats (but won't kill) everybody— probably

Jack made me write that

Joey swung his head back and forth dejectedly as he read. "Geez," he said softly, "I forgot. Chester could eat my praying mantis, too."

He slumped onto my bed and spotted *Shiloh*, which I had finished last night. Absentmindedly, he began flipping the pages.

"What's this about?" he asked.

"A boy who finds a dog," I answered.

Joey perked up. "Does he get to keep him?"

"Read it and see," I said with a smile.

He stared at the cover. A friendly beagle stared back. "Yeah," he said, "I will." He wandered out of my room, gripping the book.

Joey and Jack were alike, but so different. Evil Jack. Innocent Joey. Jack-the-jock. Joey-the-artist. Jack read survival books. Joey loved ones about animals. And fantasy. He'd read the whole Narnia series twice.

If I'd had a sister, would she have been like me? I definitely wasn't anything like Mom.

Mom. The memory of her news hit me like a rock.

"Hey, Iz." Logan, without all the books, was peeking timidly into my room. Logan is not normally shy. "Can I come in?"

"Sure." I slumped in my desk chair.

Logan flopped onto my bed and filled it up. Last year he'd been my height, but sometime, when none of us was looking, he grew an extra four or five inches.

"So," he said, kicking off his sneakers, as though he planned to stay a while, "you going to tell me what's wrong?"

"Wrong?" I asked.

"Earlier," he said. "When your face looked like chicken pox."

"Oh." I sighed. "It's Mom. She's not going to travel with her job anymore."

"Well, hey!" said Logan. "That's cool. Right?"

"Wrong."

"Look," he answered. "I know she can be kind of obsessed sometimes, but she can't be *that* bad."

Logan gave me this sort of pleading, give-her-a-break look. I knew he was thinking about his real dad, the one he didn't have anymore because he had dropped dead of a heart attack when Logan was five.

"She's always been nice to me," said Logan. "And she's great looking . . . I mean, you know . . . she's so together. And she's an awesome cook." Logan kept selling. "Besides, don't you want to get out of this crazy house sometimes?"

"It wouldn't be *sometimes*," I said. "It would be *all* the time."

"What!" Logan sat straight up on my bed. "No way."

"She wants me to live with her, *permanently*."

Logan stared at me as though I'd just told him he had to give away his drums.

"That . . . that's not fair," he sputtered.

"No kidding," I said, sitting straight. I slammed my fist onto my desk. "Well, I'm not going!"

"You're not?"

"No, goofball," I said, feeling all warm and happy inside that it mattered to him. I thought back to the awful year when none of them even spoke to me—the year I would have killed to live with Mom.

"But, Logan," I asked, sagging back into my chair, "how do I tell her that?"

Logan's face went blank. He chewed on his thumbnail. "Iz," he said finally, his voice soft and sad. "I have no clue."

I could see this was humongous to him—just like it was to me. I loved my mom. Thinking about Logan's dad dying made me feel how much. But living with her? No way.

That would mean no Dad or Alice, except to visit. No Logan, Jack, and Joey. A smile tugged at the corners of my mouth. No animal house crammed with mantises, fish, snakes, crabs, turtles, crickets, chameleons, and hedgehogs. No more listening to drums or to Jack and Joey arguing. No road rage trips or praying mantis parties. No unmade beds.

"What's funny?" asked Logan.

"Oh." I shrugged. "I was just thinking of all the fun I'd miss."

I flipped through the pages of my word calendar, wondering if it would be the most exciting thing I'd have to do at Mom's house. That, and getting Claire back. After all, no more Logan would mean no more Claire, the flirt queen.

"I think I'll e-mail Claire," I said, seriously doubting that she'd answer me. "She's good at figuring stuff out."

"Who?" said Logan.

Was he for real?

"The girl who memorizes every word you say and drools on you," I answered.

"No, she doesn't," said Logan, his whole face flushing scarlet.

"See?" I sneered. "You *do* know who she is."

"Do not," he muttered.

"Do, too," I teased.

"Check it out," we both said together, "we sound like Jack and Joey!"

After Logan left, I e-mailed Claire.

Subj: Help!

Date: 4/13/02 5:57:13 PM Eastern Daylight Time

From: Izbeck

To: clairevoyant

hey Claire

sorry I yelled at u

Im majerly stressed Help. Pleeze?

U always know what 2 do

moms quitting her gr8 job & taking an ok job–so I can

LIVE WITH HER! What do i do??!!!??

yr friend   Iz

ps   I need a free pet–u no–1 that can look after itself

for 3 days

any ideas?

Subject: Re: Help!

Date: 4/13/02 10:09:17 PM Eastern Daylight Time

From: clairevoyant

To: Izbeck

Yo Iz,

Im sorry i blew up at u 2

OMG! u wont get 2 live w/Logan! can i take yr place :-)

Ok—ur not going 2 like my advice but here it is

talk to yr mom! tell her the truth. u dont have to say shes

boring—just that u love yr new family.

stop shaking yr head. I can c u.

u have no choice

friends 4ever Claire

ps remenber mi crazy aunt nora? well she has a crazy

parot named Elvis & she's moving 2 a absolootly no pets

apartment & has 2 find him a home. Shes frantick i bet

shed even pay 4 food and vet bills

do u want me 2 call her?

Subject: Elvis
Date: 4/13/02 10:18:03 PM Eastern Daylight Time
From: Izbeck
To: clairevoyant

YES!!!!!!!
luv, Iz

I'm getting a parrot!

And Claire's still my friend!

Double *yes!*

I was bummed about her solution to Mom, though. Even if Claire happened to be right, it was easy enough for her to say. She's not the one who'd have to tell my mother that I love a house full of praying mantises better than her.

Maybe Dad would tell her. I shut down my computer, and went to find him. He and Alice were sitting at the dining room table—the one we never use, with a million pieces of paper spread around them. Was Dad working on his ad project?

Was Alice grading papers? Who knew, but they looked about as happy as two dragons with headaches, so I slipped back upstairs.

In my room, I pulled on the too-big T-shirt I love to sleep in, and padded across the hall to brush my teeth. The lights were off in Jack and Joey's room. Were they asleep? Had they forgotten Operation Cricket already?

"*Charp.*" I heard a lame cricket imitation, then giggles.

I stuck my head into their room. The hall light oozed in enough for me to see both of them in their beds. "Hey, guys," I whispered. "How's Chester? Ready for action?"

"Totally," said Jack, popping up from under his covers.

"I'm giving him a pep talk," said Joey, holding up his bug box for me to see.

"Good luck."

"Thanks, Iz," they answered together.

Jack, I thought, smiling, is nowhere near as bad as he thinks.

I tiptoed quietly back across the hall, and crawled into bed. Lying in the dark, I thought about the great Get-a-Dog plan. Would it work?

Then I thought about Mom. Would Dad tell her that I wanted to stay with him, or would he make me do it? How long did I have before she'd be back? A week?

Do normal girls lie awake at night asking themselves questions?

I closed my eyes and tried not to think about anything.

Stuff kept showing up in my head anyway.

How late would Joey have to stay up before he could sneak Chester into Dad and Alice's room?

And what was so crazy about Elvis?

GOod NEws, ReALLy Bad NEws

The night of the cricket was a disaster. Not because the plan didn't work, but because it worked too well.

At breakfast the next morning, Dad, Alice, and Joey looked like zombies. Joey could barely keep his head out of his cereal bowl. Dad and Alice had bloodshot eyes, but they weren't droopy and yawning like Joey. They were mad.

"Joey," Dad growled. "Your cricket's still in our room. Find it!"

"Do you know what time Rob and I got to sleep?" Alice asked through clenched teeth.

"No," said Joey meekly.

"Never!" Alice barked.

Dad never growls. Alice never barks. Who knew that zero sleep would turn them both into animals?

Logan grabbed Joey up out of his chair. "Come on," he said. "I'll help you find him."

"Me, too." I jumped up and trotted after them. Rounding the corner to Dad and Alice's bedroom, I slammed into Jack.

"Hey," he grumbled. "Watch where you're going!"

"Sorry," I said. "Follow me."

As soon as we entered the bedroom, we gasped.

"Wow!" exclaimed Jack. "Would you take a look at this?"

Every piece of furniture was jerked away from the wall. Table lamps sat on the floor. Stacks of books had been pulled off the bookshelves. Desk drawers emptied all over the place. It looked like a robbery.

Logan's jaw dropped.

"Joey," I said. "What happened?"

"They didn't go to bed until after two," he said

softly. Then he thrust his chest out and raised his voice. "But Chester and I stayed up! We waited."

"Until two o'clock in the morning?" I asked.

"Yeah," said Joey.

"Why?" asked Logan.

"Taxes," Joey answered.

"Taxes?"

"Yeah," said Joey. "Something about taxes being due. Mom said Rob should have started them sooner. Rob said Mom should've. Then they admitted they both should've."

It's April, I thought. Isn't that when Mom says income taxes get filed? I looked at the calendar on Alice's desk. Today was the fourteenth. Of course. Dad and Alice's income taxes were due tomorrow.

Dad and Alice never planned ahead.

"Did they finish?" I asked.

"No," said Joey, sadly.

"Who cares," said Jack. "What happened to the cricket?"

"When they finally got into bed, I sneaked Chester in," Joey answered. "Then I went to bed.

Maybe an hour later, I don't know, sometime, Mom woke me up. 'Joey, find your cricket,' she said. 'We can't sleep.'"

Joey collapsed on Dad and Alice's unmade bed. Then he curled up in a little ball like he was going back to sleep. "We tried to find him," he mumbled with his eyes closed, "but he wouldn't chirp with the lights on. They sent me back to my room. I guess he chirped some more after I left."

"This is great!" exclaimed Jack. "GAD works! Tonight we'll turn Tiggy loose. Tomorrow"—he did his hiss-and-coil imitation again—"snake night."

"I dunno," said Logan, wrinkling his face in a goofy way.

"Just so I don't have to do it," said Joey, with his eyes still closed.

"What do you mean, 'I dunno!'" shouted Jack. "You dorks! This was the plan."

"Jack!" I exploded. "Use your puny brain. They'll be up again tonight finishing their taxes. People who don't pay taxes go to prison. Besides, another night without sleep and they'll freak."

"Right," said Jack.

"Prison?" Joey's eyes popped open.

"You don't go to prison for paying late," Logan assured him. Only he didn't sound positive.

"Okay," I said. "Maybe no prison, but they will freak. They'll kill us. They have to go to work today . . . and tomorrow . . . *and* file taxes. They need sleep."

"Me, too," muttered Joey, closing his eyes again.

"If they kill us, they'll go to prison," said Jack. "Then we'll never get a dog."

"Shut up, Jack," said Logan. "You may be right, though—about our plan. This is what we planned."

Geez, I thought. Sometimes all three of them could be such dummies.

"Let . . . me . . . explain . . . this." I said it slowly, as if I were teaching three-year-olds. "We want our weird pets to annoy them, so that a dog will look easy, you know, inviting. We don't want them so sleep-deprived that they're too mad to want *anything*. Especially not when they're already stressed about taxes."

82

And, I thought, especially when I've got to ask Dad to be the heavy for me with Mom, but I didn't say that.

"So we wimp out, and don't get a dog," said Jack, pouting.

"*Gotcha!*" shouted Logan, diving into the far corner of the room and coming up with a closed fist. "I got Chester!"

Joey's eyes popped open again. He staggered across the room and took Chester from Logan, then stumbled out of the room. Two long wiggling antennae reached up through his loosely closed fist, feeling the air.

"Logan! Iz!" Alice called up the steps. "Your bus is coming."

"Okay!" we yelled back.

"Did you find Chester?" Dad shouted.

"Yes!"

"Well, hooray," answered Dad more quietly.

At school, Claire was waiting by my locker.

"I called Aunt Nora this morning," she said, the second I rounded the corner.

I hurried over. "And?"

"Well," she paused, beaming at me like a giant sunray. "There's good news and bad news!"

"Yeah?" I asked uneasily. "What's the good news?"

"She'd love to give you Elvis!" she exclaimed, still glowing. "You can have his cage, his toys, everything, and she'll pay for all his food and vet bills—forever."

My heart pumped two extra beats. *Bump. Bump.* "And the bad news?"

Claire struggled to hold back the grin that was splitting her face, but it was like trying to keep the bang inside a lighted firecracker.

"Elvis is a very unusual bird." She snickered.

"How unusual?" I asked, testily.

"Verrrrrry unusual," said Claire, rolling her eyes.

"Claire," I shouted. "For Pete's sake! Tell me about the stupid parrot!"

Kids ambling down the hall on their way to class turned and stared.

"Sorry, Iz," she said, still grinning. "Elvis is just *really* weird. Aunt Nora says he's an ornery old coot, but she loves him. She swears he reminds her of Uncle Lester."

"Who's Uncle Lester?"

"Her husband—my uncle. He was an ornery old coot, too, but he died. I think Elvis's bad habits remind her of—"

"What *are* his bad habits?" I interrupted impatiently.

"Uncle Lester's?"

"No!" I screamed. "The bird's!"

"Look," said Claire matter-of-factly. She had finally stopped grinning. "He's not very friendly. Aunt Nora's worried he may not 'take to you.'"

"Yeah?" I wasn't worried—I'm great with animals. "What else?"

"He squawks until you let him out of his cage."

"Okay, so I'll let him out."

Claire's grin exploded back onto her face. "That's when he goes to the bathroom!"

I stared at her. What did that mean? Did he have a litter box or something, or did he just fly all around the house dropping bird-doo everywhere?

"He's got a cactus," Claire continued, gleefully. "Aunt Nora says it's big—about three feet high—and covered with poop. Well, actually it was Uncle Lester's cactus, but Elvis sort of claimed it. It's the only place he'll go." Claire smirked. "Aunt Nora says you can have the cactus."

"Good grief," I muttered.

But the more I thought about it, the more perfect it sounded. GAD needed new ideas—ones that didn't keep Dad and Alice awake. What if I took Elvis *without* the cactus? Would he poop all over the house? What if I left him in the kitchen? Alice might not mind dirty dishes in the sink, but bird doo?

I laughed out loud.

Claire giggled.

"I'll take him," I said.

"Really?" asked Claire, her eyes wide.

Suddenly I realized that I'd seen so little of Claire lately, she was totally clueless about the Get-a-Dog plan.

The buzzer, signaling one minute until class, went off.

"Yeah," I said hurriedly. "I want him. I'll explain later."

Claire beamed. "I'll bring him by your house after school," she said over her shoulder, as she turned and hurried to class.

"No!" I tried to call after her. "I'll come get him!"

But she was already gone. Good-bye, regular Claire. Hello, barf.

The flirt queen was coming to my house.

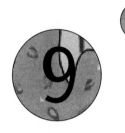

Blue Hair

On the bus ride home from school, I stared out the window and played twenty questions with myself.

What was I supposed to do about Mom? Should I talk to Dad about it tonight, or wait until he finished his taxes? *Duh.* Of course I should wait. But I didn't want to.

And how was I going to convince Jack, Joey, and Logan that their all-night, hyper-hedgehog plan was a mistake? Somehow, I'd have to sell them a better idea. Hopefully, Elvis.

Was I really about to be the owner of a crazy parrot?

And what about Claire? If she showed up acting like a moron around Logan, would I get mad, or just throw up on her?

88

When I got home, Jack was standing at the front door, punching Joey in the chest with his baseball glove and screaming, "You idiot!"

"Hey," said Joey defensively. "I said I was sorry."

"You got that right!" shouted Jack, bolting out the door and slamming it behind him.

Logan rounded the corner from the kitchen and gave Joey a friendly shove. "Relax," he said. "Jack'll get over it. Let's grab a snack and work on the pet plan."

While we all stared into the open refrigerator, trying to make up our minds, Joey explained to me, "Jack's coach called and said there'd be an extra practice today. I forgot to tell him."

Jack is the star pitcher on his baseball team, and thanks to him, the Sports Warehouse Warthogs were undefeated, 6–0.

Joey sounded pretty sad that he'd blown it. "I was reading your book," he said, "and I forgot."

We all grabbed something to eat and headed upstairs to my room to revise GAD, Part Two. I was sorry that Jack might be in trouble for getting to practice late, but I was glad he wouldn't be home. I'd have a better chance of destroying the parents-without-sleep plan.

Asking for new animals gradually, Part One, hadn't exactly gone according to plan, but at least we'd all managed to come up with an assortment of pets. One new hermit crab, a cricket, a snake. And crazy Elvis was on his way. Part Two, turning creatures loose to do wild and icky stuff, had worked too well. It had turned Dad and Alice mean. Not to mention prison possibilities.

Right now, I was betting on Elvis to be the shining star of GAD, Part Two.

I popped the top on my Dr. Pepper can. *Fsssssss.* Nelson, perched on my window curtain, cocked his little green head.

Logan sprawled across my bed, licking the centers out of a stack of Oreos, while Joey sucked on a cherry Popsicle. My room smelled yummy.

"Where's your daily mealworm snack?" I asked.

Joey stuck his red-dye-#2 tongue out at me.

"Okay," said Logan, prying open another Oreo. "What's next?"

"Elvis," I answered, proudly.

"Presley?"

"Idiots," I muttered. Then, I explained every-thing to them about Aunt Nora's parrot.

"Awesome!" cried Joey.

"Claire's coming over?" asked Logan.

Ggukk! I gagged on my Dr. Pepper. If Logan thought that Claire coming over was more inter-esting than a feathered, ornery old coot with freaky bathroom habits, I didn't want to guess what that meant.

I ignored him.

"So," I asked, "what do you think? About let-ting Elvis loose?" I added.

"It beats staying up until two," said Joey. He yawned so big, his mouth looked like a black hole, dyed red.

"Hey, I know!" cried Logan, wiping his choco-late hands on my sheets. "Sometimes if I feed Tiggy a bunch of leftovers instead of cat food, her BMs come out like soup."

"Whoa," I said. "What would happen if we fed everybody rich food?"

"Bombs away!" Joey shrieked. "We could launch a number-two attack!"

Logan fell back laughing. Suddenly, his eyes lit up and he doubled over into a second fit of laughter. "It *is* GAD!" he gasped, before doubling up into another spasm. "Get it? GAD!" he wheezed. "Get it?"

We stared at him.

"We don't get it," I said, swigging a swallow of soda.

"GAD," he guffawed. "Get it? Give Animals Diarrhea!"

Logan rolled off the bed, *blam!* He hit the floor, still laughing.

I spewed my mouthful of Dr. Pepper halfway across the room.

Joey roared.

The doorbell rang.

"It's Elvis!" we cried together.

I jumped up and flew down the stairs to beat Logan to the door. When I opened it, two surprises greeted me.

Surprise #1 was Elvis. I'd pictured a big parrot,

at least the size of a hawk, with lots of bright, different-colored feathers, and a majestic look. Instead, Elvis was a small, totally green bird, no bigger than a blue jay. He was cute.

Surprise #2 was Claire. Her long blond hair was one of the colors I'd expected Elvis to be. It was blue! Bright blue. The color of crayons. Or parrots.

"Do you think Logan will like it?" she asked, nervously.

I was speechless.

"He'll love Elvis," I said, finally.

Claire's chin began to quiver. She was going to cry.

Behind us came the thumping bumps of Logan and Joey bounding down the stairs.

Claire shoved the bird toward my face. "Here!" she said and turned to escape.

"Hey!" Logan exclaimed. "Man, look at you. That is cool."

Claire stopped. "Really?" she said anxiously.

"It'll wash out."

"It's awesome!" said Joey, gazing openmouthed

93

at Claire, as if she were Spiderman and Princess Leia, all rolled into one.

"Yeah," said Logan. "It looks good."

Claire beamed.

Logan reached for Elvis, but he squawked and flapped his wings. Claire held on to him by his feet.

"I walked here," she said. "I couldn't carry his cage. It's pretty heavy."

"I'll help you," Logan offered.

"You will?" Claire cooed, lowering her eyes and looking helpless.

It wouldn't have surprised me one bit if she'd said, "Oooooo Logan, you are sooooo strong."

Before I could even say *barf*, they were strolling down the front walk, off to Claire's house. Joey ran after them.

"Can I carry Elvis?" he shouted.

I stood in the open doorway. Stunned. Birdless, brotherless, and totally best friendless.

Back in my room, I sprawled on my bed. "I want a dog," I told Nelson, hoping he wouldn't notice that I was about to cry. But he was too busy scoping a tiny spider to care. Glitz eyed me and swam around in worried circles, so I pinched some fish food out of the box beside my bed, and dropped the flakes into his water. He darted up, popping open-mouthed from flake to flake, gobbling them as fast as he could.

Maybe that should have made me feel needed, but it didn't.

I slogged down to the basement and flipped on the light to see if Tiggy was awake. No sign of her.

Sitting cross-legged on the concrete floor in front of her sofa cushion, I whistled softly. Still nothing.

Then I hummed a lullaby that Mom had sung to me when I was little. I felt a little tug at my heart, remembering that Mom *still* sang that song to me. Not a peep from Tiggy, though.

Idiot, I told myself. You don't sing lullabies to wake someone up. I thought about banging on the overhead pipes, but that would be too noisy. Sudden racket made Tiggy scream. So I chanted rap lyrics.

A few seconds later, a shiny black nose on the

tip of a furry pointed snout peeked out from the hole in the cushion.

"Tiggy," I whispered gratefully, reaching forward slowly to let her smell my hands. Her nose vibrated, sniffing. Then her glossy black eyes peered out, looking like tiny polished marbles, but gleaming with life. I wanted to hug her.

Never hug a hedgehog.

I remembered the first time I ever picked her up. The sharpness of her prickly spines had startled me, but compared to what happened next, that was nothing. She had sniffed for a second, and then she'd begun licking my hand like a demon—totally possessed. The next thing I knew she was foaming at the mouth, and flinging saliva all over her back, coating her spines with gross, bubbly stuff.

"Rabies!" I'd shouted, frantically handing her back to Logan, who was laughing.

"Relax," he said. "It's something hedgehogs do. It's called self-anointing."

"Why?" I asked.

"Don't know." He shook his head. "I think it's how she imprints your scent so she'll know you next time. Or maybe it's some weird kind of protection—in case you turn out to be a hedgehog assassin."

Right now, back in my basement, I felt more like a Claire assassin.

I cupped my hands in front of the opening in the cushion. Tiggy waddled to my waiting palms and snuggled into them as if I were a nest. Gently, I eased her onto my lap and began stroking the soft patch of fur between her eyes.

How did Claire get blue hair so fast? I wondered. It was blond this morning.

Quietly, I sang Mom's lullaby. Maybe I *did* belong at her house.

Tiggy made cute little chirpy-purring sounds, and went back to sleep.

Wham! Upstairs the front door banged, followed by the thumping and scuffling of feet.

"Iz!" three voices shouted together. "Where are you? We're back!"

Tenderly, I placed Tiggy back inside her hole, and trudged upstairs.

Logan, Joey, and Claire were already in my room, positioning a huge cage into one corner.

"It needs to be higher," motioned Claire.

I stared at her insane blue hair.

Logan lifted the cage onto my bed.

"Excuse me," I said, "but I do need somewhere to sleep, you know."

Claire and Logan whirled around. "Iz!" they cried, happily.

"Where were you?" asked Logan.

"We thought you were coming with us," said Claire.

Believe it or not, they both sounded like they honestly missed me.

"Here, Elvis. Here, boy," Joey called into the empty cage on my bed. There was no sign of a bird, but the cage contained a huge wooden box with a parrot-sized doorway cut into it.

I eyed the open mesh bottom of the cage and said, "Uh, guys? How about getting that off my bed?" Just because Aunt Nora claimed Elvis went to the bathroom only on a cactus, didn't mean I believed it.

"Oh," said Logan looking around the room for a better spot. "How about your desk?"

"I'll get newspapers to line the bottom," said Claire. "If you'll tell me where they are," she crooned at Logan.

Joey pointed to the piles of loose papers on my desk and said, "Iz doesn't need newspaper. Just put it on that."

"Fine," I muttered, hoping nothing important was on top.

Logan picked up the cage and set it on top of my messy desk. I could swear he held it in the air forever so Claire could see his muscles.

EXPLoDING BiRD POOP

Aunt Nora's hunch was absolutely right. Elvis did not "take to me." I spent the entire week showing that stupid bird what a caring person I was, but he didn't buy it. Not for a second.

Tuesday:

Elvis: wouldn't come out of his box, except, just like we'd been warned, to go to the bathroom. He pitched what Aunt Nora called a "hissie-bird fit." He squawked his little green tail feathers off, but if I reached in to take him out of his cage, he'd vanish, flapping and screeching, back into his box.

Finally, I gave up and hid Nelson. I sure didn't need for Elvis to "take to" my praying mantis. Then I left Elvis's door open. He zoomed out, swooping wildly in search of his missing cactus. Shooing him toward the kitchen was a joke. No amount of shouting and arm waving would make him leave my room.

Eventually, he hovered, flapped his wings, and settled onto my bedside lamp, probably because it was tall and green, and deposited a buttful of bird-doo on the light bulb. Clearly pleased, he zipped straight back to his hide-box, banged around for a while—to sound bigger, I guess—and finally shut up.

GAD: Logan, Joey, Jack, and I all agreed: no hyper-hedgehog night. That also meant: no prison. Tiggy and Shellie started diets guaranteed to give them the runs.

Dad and Alice: finished their taxes way after the rest of us had gone to sleep, so I didn't talk to Dad about living with Mom. Besides, I was too busy brushing Logan's Oreo crumbs out of my bed.

Wednesday:

Elvis: same as Tuesday, except Jack hung out with him after baseball practice. He seemed to "take to" Jack. Who knows what he did while I was at school, but I'm guessing he squawked a lot. He didn't go to the bathroom in his cage, though. *He saved it.*

Joey: has a spiral notebook that he's drawing all our animals in.

Claire: waved to me at school, but I pretended not to see her—which is a joke, because how can you not see blue hair? But until she gets over this Logan thing, I just can't deal with her.

GAD: Jack came up with a plan that he hadn't clued anyone else in on. Before dinner, he hid Logan's snake in one of Alice's big cooking pots. She began filling the pot with water to boil the spaghetti in. Then she saw Hiss. Calmly, she removed the pot, poured out the water, and called, "Logan! Come get your snake."

Logan: retrieved Hiss, then went ballistic at Jack. "You idiot!" he screamed. "You could've gotten him cooked!"

Dad: was exhausted from two late nights of taxes, plus two workdays on his ad project, so I nixed the I-don't-want-to-move-in-with-Mom talk.

Tiggy and Shellie: had loose hedgehog and turtle droppings, but no runny ones yet.

Thoughts of Mom: kept me awake asking myself how I'd get out of living with her, without hurting her feelings. And since I was lying in the dark asking myself questions anyway, I spent a bunch of time wondering if I should tell Claire she's acting like a fool. After that, I spent a little more time thinking of words that the letters in *fool* could stand for. About midnight, I hit on it. FOOL: Flirts Obnoxiously Over Logan. I laughed out loud. Then, I tossed and turned and kicked a few more chocolate crumbs out of my bed. Finally, hoping he'd learn to like me, I talked sweet-and-soft to Elvis until I fell asleep.

Thursday:

Elvis: see Wednesday.

Claire (and her blue hair): showed up after school to visit Elvis. At least that's what she said. (Ha!) Logan gave her an animal tour. When he handed her his garter snake, she squealed and dropped it. Logan, her hero, smiled protectively and picked it up. Later, in Jack's room, she closed her eyes and daintily lifted Killer up by his tail, but when he wiggled, she jerked, and the tail came off in her hand. Detached. Totally disconnected. Lizards can do that to escape their enemies, and then grow back new ones. We looked it up. That's when we discovered that Killer isn't even a chameleon. He's an anole, which is a lizard that can change colors. And let go of his tail. *Erk.*

Claire's face (when she had Killer's tail in her hand): twisted, horrified, and Ugly with a capital *U.*

Jack: thinks Killer anole sounds majorly wimpy, so he's going to keep calling him a chameleon.

Shellie and Tiggy: had diarrhea all over our kitchen floor. Alice didn't freak. "Logan! Joey!" she called. "Come clean this up." I began to suspect that GAD would soon be history.

Dad: just wanted to "relax." He fell asleep in front of the TV. So, no Mom-talk, again. Fine with me. I'd worried so long, I didn't want to discuss it anymore. I just wanted it to go away.

Friday:

Elvis: I'd spent every afternoon and half of each night cooing and coaxing that stupid bird, and he wouldn't even come out of his box. Jack, on the other hand, could stroll in and Elvis would hop over like an old friend, touching Jack's hand with his beak—which was always wet because Elvis had a runny nose. Even Jack couldn't get him out of my room, though. And I've learned to clean my lamp before dark, because when I turn on the bulb, it heats up. Cooked bird droppings smell like you know what.

Captain Hook: died. Jack fed him a peanut-butter-and-jelly sandwich. This was not part of GAD. It wasn't even part of Jack trying to be evil. The chart I'd made listed hermit crabs as loving peanut butter and fruit, so Jack fixed him a treat. What my chart overlooked was: no soggy bread, because it can plug up a crab's gills and suffocate him.

Poor Jack. And, especially, poor Captain Hook.

Shellie and Tiggy: We canceled the super-rich

food plan, so Shellie was back to normal, but Tiggy still had the runs.

Dad: I decided to wait until Saturday to talk to him. One more day couldn't hurt.

Mom: called. She'd be home Monday. For good. She couldn't wait to see me. And "make moving plans."

Saturday:

Tiggy: still had diarrhea. And she wasn't her hyper self. At all. She nestled in my lap, and snuggled down deep when I rubbed between her eyes, but she didn't make happy noises. She didn't make any noises. I told Logan he needed to give her some cheese or something. . .I don't know. . . something that would stop up hedgehog plumbing.

Jack: pitched a no-hitter today. We all went to his game—right after Dad whipped up his Saturday morning special of omelets and bacon.

Joey: finished his notebook with all our animals in it. It's awesome. Captain Hook's there, even though he's dead, because Joey had already drawn him. And Killer still has his tail, for the same reason. I wish *I* could draw.

Claire: showed up to see Elvis (double Ha!), but we were all at Jack's baseball game. She left a dopey note: *Sorry 1 missed you guys!!! Do you need any help with Elvis? Call me! Claire.* All her *i*'s were dotted with hearts.

Elvis: belongs to Jack now. I gave him away so Jack wouldn't be so sad about Captain Hook dying, and because, when I got back from the baseball game, Elvis was squawking to go potty, so I opened his cage. He made a beeline for my lamp, perched over the lightbulb—which I'd left on the whole time I was gone—and *poweee!* The bulb exploded when the bird-doo hit it. Broken glass and fresh poop flew in fifty directions. Elvis shot back into his hide-box like a bullet. He banged and slammed around for two hours before he finally lightened up. Serves him right. Jack went to Aunt Nora's and got the cactus. Then he helped me wash my sheets, walls, carpet, lamp, goldfish bowl, and miscellaneous everything.

Dad: finally. I talked to him about Mom. He was in his garden, pulling up last year's dead plants so he could get ready for this year's. He smelled like dirt and sweat, which is a good and bad smell, both at the same time. "Mom wants me to live with her," I said. Dad froze over his dead pepper plants and stared at me. I explained all about her job change. For a while, he didn't say anything, just ripped six-foot-tall okra stalks out of the dirt and slammed them onto the ground like the pro wrestlers you see on TV. That's when I found out there were two things that freaked out casual Dad—no sleep, and Mom making plans about me without talking to him first. "Will I talk to your Mom?" he said through clenched teeth. "You bet I'll talk to your Mom." Then he got a scared look on his face. "Iz," he said. "Would you rather live with her?" "Heck, no," I said. Then he hugged me, dirt, sweat, and all.

Sunday:

GAD: Logan, Jack, Joey, and I all met in my room to review the success of GAD, and to decide what to do next. We unanimously agreed it was a total bust. The noisy-pet-while-you're-sleeping idea only made Dad and Alice mean. The pets-with-diarrhea plan made Tiggy sick, and gave the rest of us huge, nasty-smelling messes to mop. And we couldn't turn them all loose at the same time because they'd eat each other. I was for letting them run free on alternate days. Jack wanted to take turns putting each of them in Dad and Alice's bed—starting with Hiss. Joey pushed hard for more pets. Logan wanted to stop arguing and go play his drums. We gave up.

Tiggy: seemed better. She purred a little while I stroked the soft fur on her tummy and hummed Mom's lullaby. Logan took her to his room. I heard him talking to her for hours.

Claire: IM-ed me while I was online: Y R U avoiding me?

I signed off like I hadn't seen it.

Alice: stuck her head in my room and said, "Can we talk?" She sat down on my unmade bed without noticing it. I had to love her for that. "I know how much your mother must want you to

109

live with her," she said. An awful feeling seized me. Did Alice want me gone? Her gaze drifted around the room, looking for a place to land. When it landed on Nelson, she smiled. "I know how much your mom wants you," she repeated, "because I know how much *I* want you." Wow. I had no clue what to say, so I murmured, "Thanks," but I loved the warm glow spreading inside me. Then she lightened up and said, "Besides, you can't go off and leave me with all these guys. I'd go nuts!" I laughed. Alice stood and hugged me. "You are very lucky to have so many people who love you," she whispered.

Me: I slept great. No squawking Elvis. Clean sheets meant no cookie crumbs. Dad was going to handle Mom. Lots of people loved me.

Monday:
Tiggy died.

PURPLe KeTCHUP

Logan had found Tiggy after dinner, in the basement, still curled up in the hole in her sofa cushion. When he didn't come right back upstairs with her, I went to see if everything was okay.

Logan sat on the hard, concrete floor, holding the cute prickly ball of fur and spines that was Tiggy.

"Is she better?" I asked, afraid.

Logan didn't answer.

I felt a hard lump in my throat. Hyper Tiggy wasn't moving.

Logan looked up at me. "Oh, Iz," he said.

I saw tears in his eyes.

"No," I whispered.

"She's dead." His voice cracked.

Joey and Jack thumped noisily down the basement steps. At the bottom, they froze, staring at Tiggy. And at the tears their big brother couldn't hold back.

"Is she—?" Joey couldn't finish.

I nodded.

Logan slumped, head down. Jack, Joey, and I stood, staring.

There was no question. We all knew we had killed her.

Dad and Alice tried to cheer us up.

"Let's go away next weekend," said Dad.

Was that Dad's answer to everything? Was that what he'd said when Mom asked for a divorce?

"Pick a place," he continued. "Any place. We can take Tiggy somewhere special and bury her there. The mountains. The beach. You name it. We can give her the best funeral any hedgehog ever had."

"I bet she'd love the mountains," said Alice. "How about that little cove with the lake where we hiked last fall? Remember how beautiful the

112

leaves were, and how all the squirrels were scurrying around getting ready for winter"—Alice looked around the room at each of us, smiling gently—"and the deer that Joey spotted right before she bounded into the woods? Remember?"

None of us could look at each other, but I knew we were all feeling the same thing. Guilt . . . and shame.

I wondered if Dad and Alice would be so nice if they knew why Tiggy died. Would we ever tell them?

"I can't go," said Jack, his voice barely a squeak. "I've got a baseball game."

"Oh, right," said Dad. "Well, then, we can find someplace closer."

"The lake at the park," suggested Alice. "Right under the big oak with the—"

"I'm going to bury her in the backyard," said Logan, flatly. "Tonight."

It was a short ceremony. Nobody said much. After Dad and Alice had gone back into the house, the four of us each told Tiggy how sorry we were.

Joey placed a flat rock on top of the freshly dug dirt. He had carefully drawn *TIGGY* on it in permanent black marker.

"Iz!" called Alice from the house. "Telephone."

It was Mom.

"Sweetheart," she said. "I'm home."

"Great, Mom. How was your flight?" I asked, wondering if she could tell from my voice that I'd been crying.

"Oh, not bad," she answered, sounding tired. "I'm a little jet-lagged, of course. But I'll be good as new tomorrow. Can you come for dinner?"

"Have you talked to Dad?" I asked, nervously.

"I have," she snapped. Then, softer, "Eliz—, I mean Iz. We need to talk. Just you and me. Okay? I haven't seen you in so long. I'd really love it if you'd spend the week with me. We don't have to decide anything permanent right away."

I didn't know what to say. So for about an eternity I didn't say anything. If I went for a week, would she own me? Like when we learned about squatter's rights in history? Did I want to spend a week with her? No. I'd miss home. Yeah? What

114

exactly would I miss? The Get-a-Dog plan was as dead as Tiggy. And seeing Logan, Jack, and Joey only reminded me of the dumb, stupid, horrible thing we'd all done that killed her.

"Sure, Mom," I said. "I'll come for a week."

Tuesday, after school, I went to Mom's with enough clothes to last me until Sunday. No more.

Dinner was hamburgers and French fries. And purple ketchup! I couldn't believe my eyes.

I plopped down at Mom's beautifully polished dining room table, set with elegant china, linen napkins, and silver, and stared at the plastic squeeze bottle. It was as out of place as a mutt at a fancy dog show.

"Purple ketchup?" I asked, in dismay. How had Mom made the move from Burgundy reduction sauce to purple ketchup?

"Do you like it?" she asked. "I hear it's the latest thing in kids' products."

I picked it up and squeezed purple goop onto my fine china plate. It clashed totally with the delicate, hand-painted, coral-colored birds. This was

115

crazy. So not Mom. Here she was doing stupid stuff, buying tropical fish and insanely dyed ketchup, and for what? For me?

I didn't know whether to laugh or cry.

Suddenly, it hit me. Something awful. Hadn't I done stupid stuff to get a dog? And here was Mom, doing equally brainless things to get me. No. Not equally. Her idea wasn't nearly as dumb as mine. After all, what was purple ketchup compared to murder?

Another thought smacked me right between the eyes. Wasn't Claire's blue hair and dumb flirting the same thing? Wasn't she just trying to get Logan?

I was as stupid as Claire. No. I was a lot stupider.

Suddenly, I'd lost my appetite.

"Well," said Mom, sounding disappointed, "don't eat it if you don't want to."

Halfheartedly, I picked up a French fry, dipped it in the purple puddle on my plate, and popped it into my mouth. My brain expected it to taste like grape juice, but it was plain old tomato ketchup.

116

I chewed slowly, forced myself to swallow, and smiled.

"Yum," I lied. Not that it tasted bad. Ordinarily, it would have been delicious. And fun. But right now the tube connecting my mouth and my stomach was so clogged with guilt that food wouldn't fit.

All I could think about was everybody doing dim-witted things to get what they wanted. Only my dumb thing was beyond dim-witted. It was criminal.

Mom cleared her throat. "About what your dad told me," she said gently, jerking me back to another reality. "He said you preferred living with him." She looked directly at me, and waited, apparently expecting me to deny it. When I didn't say anything, she continued. "I'm sure that's not what you said."

"Well," I stalled. "It's not *exactly* what I said."

"I knew it!" she exclaimed. "He's in denial again. It's just like him—"

"Whoa," I said. "What's *in denial?*"

"He refuses to see the truth when it's not what

117

he wants," she answered. "And this time he's even lied about what *you* want." She balled both her hands into fists and placed them firmly on the tabletop.

"No!" I exclaimed. "He didn't lie. He—"

"Oh, sweetheart, don't defend him," she said, quickly loosening her fists and patting my arm with one hand. "I know how he changes things."

"He didn't change—"

"He thinks I forgot how much you wanted to live with me when he married Alice." She looked at me knowingly. "And it hurt me so much that you couldn't." Her voice trailed off, filled with sadness. She sat straighter. "But now you can."

I could hear Claire screaming in my head: *Tell her! Iz. Tell her the truth.* I was so confused. I did not want to hear more bad things about Dad. But I didn't want her mad at me, either. Besides, I had a whole week to tell her. I smiled lamely and choked down another purple French fry.

"Pass the ketchup," I said, forcing a laugh.

Mom beamed.

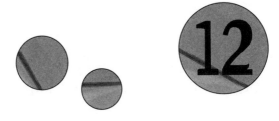

Honest, Even If It Hurts

At school on Wednesday, I looked for Claire. It wasn't hard. She was the only one in the cafeteria with blue hair.

"Hey, Claire." I tried to sound casual as I stepped behind her in line.

"*Humph,*" she snorted.

Okay. I couldn't blame her. But now that I knew I was tons stupider than she was, I was determined to patch things up.

"I thought it washed out," I said, nodding toward her hair. It did look lighter.

"I thought so, too." She slid her tray farther down the line, away from me.

I grabbed a slice of pizza and caught up with her.

"How'd you dye it so fast, anyway?" I asked. "At school you were blond. After school you were *blunette*."

Claire bit her lower lip to smother a giggle, then stomped off to a table with only one space left. She shot me a meaningful look that said, *I am sitting here and, clearly, there is no room for you.*

I sat at the next table and waited for her to finish eating. When she got up, I followed her. As she slid her empty tray onto a stack of dirty ones, she whirled around to face me and practically spit, "I know you got my IM."

I hesitated, but only for a second. "You're right," I said. "I did. I'm sorry I didn't answer it." Finally, a chance for me to be honest with *somebody*.

Claire looked stunned. Then hurt. "Why?" she asked, her face not even trying to mask the sting.

"Because I'm stupid," I said. "Can we just let it go?"

Claire studied my face, trying to read what I wouldn't tell her.

I wasn't ready yet to say how much I hated the

way she acted around Logan. I needed to take this brand new, be-honest-even-if-it-hurts program in baby steps.

"Tiggy died," I blurted.

Claire's face softened. "I know," she said. "Logan told me."

Ouch. Were they hanging out?

"Iz. I'm so sorry," she said.

"Me, too," I answered.

"I sprayed my hair." Thankfully, Claire had changed the subject. "That's how I did it so fast," she explained.

"Spray?"

"Yeah," she said. "It's supposed to wash out, but so far, it's only faded a lot." She laughed. "Logan liked it better bright blue, though. So next time I'm going to use the cream stuff."

"Next time?" I knew I sounded like a moron.

"It lasts longer, but Mom and Dad might kill me." She giggled that flirty little laugh that said, *I'll do anything for Logan.*

I guess they were going to be a thing, whether I liked it or not.

"My cousin used Kool-Aid," she continued. "But you have to add some extra ingredient, and she couldn't remember what."

Kool-Aid! I tried to imagine myself putting Kool-Aid on my already hopeless hair. Talk about Frizz City.

"It has to be sugarless, though. I do know that," said Claire. "Otherwise, something awful happens, only my cousin couldn't remember what."

I grinned. Regular Claire and I headed for class, her babbling, me listening.

It was the most normal thing in my life right now.

My week at Mom's was nice, but so peaceful it was mind-numbing. And she was trying way too hard to make me happy. Every day she made me feel worse. She wanted to redo my room. I could pick anything I wanted. Striped curtains or flowered ones? Did I need new software? Games? Clothes? Let's go shopping.

Halfway through the week, I began to suspect

that she *did* believe what Dad told her. Why else would she be trying so hard to win me?

School. Mom's. Claire's. Everywhere I went, guilt covered me like a giant cobweb, clinging, smothering. Guilt about not wanting to live with her. Guilt about not standing up for Dad. Guilt about Tiggy.

I wondered how Logan, Joey, and Jack were handling the Tiggy part.

I'd seen Logan at school, but I knew he didn't want me to bring the subject up there, and I didn't want to.

I promised myself I'd tell Dad and Alice about our stupid GAD plan as soon as I got home. Logan, Jack, and Joey might freak, but I was ready to try anything that might unloose some of this guilt.

I'd also decided to tell Mom the truth, no matter what, on Saturday. I really wanted to go to Jack's baseball game, even though this was supposed to be Mom's time. Maybe that would help her see that he was my brother, my real brother.

And that I hated missing out. Then it would be easier to tell her.

Heck, if I got on a big enough roll with my honesty kick, I might even tell Claire what a doofus she was around Logan.

I thought back to how warm and fuzzy I'd felt when Alice told me I was lucky that so many people loved me. By next weekend, that grand total would probably be zero. Was it worth it?

Saturday, I asked Mom if she would drop me at Jack's game.

"I thought we'd play tennis," she answered, apparently clueless that I might have another life.

Tennis? Now I was clueless. Did I play tennis? Did Mom play tennis?

"I signed us up for lessons," she explained, smiling warmly.

"Great, Mom," I said. "But some other time. Okay? I really want to go to Jack's baseball game."

I left Mom standing in the hall, looking like a heavy fog was rolling in, and she had no idea where it had come from. But when I called Alice to see what time Jack's game was, she said that Jack was sick. Headache and fever. Probably the flu.

Jack, sick? Jack might be too sick to go to school, but he was never too sick to play baseball. The Warthogs would be toast. I chuckled to myself—actually, they'd be bacon.

So Mom and I had our private tennis lesson, after all. And I loved it. Mom was surprisingly good—a regular jock. Who knew?

Afterward, we stopped for ice cream. *Tell her now*, said the voice in my head.

I ordered a sugar cone of something called triple fudge mudslide. Mom got a cup of pistachio. We sat outdoors at a tiny pink wrought-iron table that was supposed to make customers think they were eating ice cream way back in the fifties— before stepfamilies were even invented.

I licked my super-rich creamy chocolate and thought about what I would say. Finally, I gave it my best shot.

"Mom. Today was fun."

"It was, wasn't it?"

"Mom," I started again, "I love you."

She stopped her spoon midway to her mouth, and lowered it slowly back into her ice cream cup. "I love you, too," she said. Her guard was up.

We both knew I'd said *I love you*, but the way I'd said it meant, *I love you, but . . .*

She waited.

"I know I wanted to live with you when Dad got married. But somewhere in all the confusion and craziness, I got used to Alice and Logan and Jack and Joey. More than used to them, Mom. I love them. We have fun."

I'd said it! I felt weird—all bubbly and flat at the same time. I stared at my ice cream cone so I wouldn't have to see what Mom's face was doing.

"I love you, Mom," I repeated. "I loved our tennis lesson. I love my new fish. I want to be with you. Honest. But, just sometimes. Not all the time."

For about a century, neither of us said a word.

My ice cream started to drip down my hand, so I licked it. But still, I didn't look up.

More silence. When Mom finally spoke, her voice was strange—almost casual, as though we'd been talking about the weather.

"I've thought about getting a dog," she said. "Would you like a dog?"

Something Awful

Late Saturday night, I lay awake in my bed at Mom's house, listening to the hum of pumps and filters on my fancy new aquarium, and asking myself questions. Do I love my mother, or do I hate my mother?

I had finally gotten up the nerve to tell her that I wanted to live with Dad, and what had she done? She had bribed me! With a dog! And acted like nothing was happening! She'd said *Dad* was *in denial*. What about her!

My first reaction had been surprise, followed by disgust, then anger. How could she be that shameless? That stupid? Did she honestly think I was so incredibly shallow?

My second reaction, the one that I will never,

128

ever tell another living soul was: what kind of dog? I hated myself for even thinking it, but I *had* thought it. I added it to my growing lump of guilt.

Sunday morning, I could barely look Mom in the face. She, on the other hand, acted as if I hadn't flung my triple fudge mudslide onto the ground the day before and stomped off to the car. But we both knew that I had.

"How about blueberry pancakes?" she asked in a perfectly normal voice, while calmly pouring milk into a bowl with flour and eggs.

"No, thanks." I reached for a box of dry cereal.

"How about a bichon frise?" she asked, as though it were a side order that went with pancakes.

"A what?"

"A bichon. You know—one of those adorable little white dogs that looks kind of like a poodle."

"Mom!" I screamed, slamming the cereal box down so hard that Cheerios flew up into the air and spilled onto the counter. "Stop! Would you please just stop!? What's the matter with you!?"

129

Mom quit stirring the batter for the pancakes that I didn't even want, and stared at me.

"I don't want a dog!" I screamed some more. "I want a family! A *big* family! Why can't you understand that?"

Tears welled up in her large hazel eyes.

"I mean, I *do* want a dog," I kept going. "You *know* I want a dog. More than almost anything. But not more than Dad and Alice and Logan and Jack and Joey. Not more than that, Mom."

The tears spilled over onto her perfect face. Her face didn't contort. Her mascara didn't run. My mom looked elegant even when she cried.

I wanted to hug her. I wanted to slap her.

The rest of the day we both pretended that nothing much had happened, but the underlying tension was so heavy I could have stuffed it into trash bags and lugged it to the dumpster.

We had a quiet dinner, watched a Hallmark made-for-TV movie, and went to bed early. I lay awake asking myself, am I a good kid for being honest, or a rotten kid for hurting Mom?

130

All I could think about was this weird Australian spider I'd read about when Logan and I were looking through our library books. The female was a great mother. She built a nest for her babies and worked like crazy catching them insects to eat. And what did the little baby spiders do when they got big enough? They ate her!

No kidding. They started by nibbling her legs off . . . slowly. I guess she must hobble around on stubs for a while, but eventually the kids munch every leg until there aren't any left. When she can't move, they chow down on the rest of her.

I tossed and turned forever. Finally, I fell asleep, but I woke myself back up making a strangled, grunting noise—the kind you make when you try to scream in your sleep, but your voice won't work.

I sat straight up, sweating and panic-stricken. I'd been dreaming I was roasting one of Mom's legs on a spit and basting it with purple ketchup.

The next morning, Mom dropped me off at school.

"Tennis on Saturday?" she asked hopefully.

"Sure." I grinned back, ecstatic that her legs

131

weren't burnt, or nibbled on, or anything.

After she drove away, I remembered—what if Jack had a game Saturday? Oh, no. I was so tired of making all the wrong decisions, I wanted to cry.

"Iz!" called Claire.

"Hey, Iz." Logan walked up with her. "Sorry I missed your mom."

"Me, too," said Claire. "I haven't seen her in forever. Does she still do her wicked-witch imitation?" Claire smiled in the direction of Mom's disappearing car. "She was so funny. A little too neat for me," she added, "but fun."

I had forgotten that sometimes Mom did her wicked-witch routine when Claire spent the night.

"Are you kidding?" I said. "You know what she's like now. Boring." I thought about our quiet dinner and dull movie. "What her place needs is a dog, a cat, and a whole bunch of kids."

"Well," said Claire, "she *is* trying to fill it with one kid."

I glared at her as if she'd stabbed me. "*You* go live with her then."

"Come on," pleaded Claire. "Ease up. She's lonely. I'd turn into big-time-boring, too, if I lived alone."

Logan was standing so close to Claire, their arms touched. Now *I* felt alone.

"So," I snapped at both of them, "you think I should move out!"

"Heck, no!" Logan blurted.

"No way!" echoed Claire.

Logan slouched left, away from Claire, and studied the dirty, cracked rubber on the sides of his sneakers. "I don't know what you should do," he said quietly.

I sagged—*whoosh*—all the fight draining right out of me. "Me, either," I muttered. Logan was so nice. Did Claire know how lucky she was?

I looked at her, gazing adoringly at Logan, arms touching again. Yeah. She knew. It almost made me smile. Did that mean I was getting used to them?

"What happened to the Warthogs Saturday?" I asked, changing the subject.

"Are you kidding?" Logan snorted. "Without Jack, they didn't stand a chance."

"Is he better?" asked Claire.

"Nope," said Logan. "He's still got a fever and is coughing his fool head off. Mom's taking him to the doctor today."

Jack was sick all week. He had a dry cough that I could hear from all over the house. I told him it was way more annoying than Chester's supersized cricket chirp.

"Shut up, Iz," he grumbled, chucking his pillow at me. Then he bent double, coughing again. He sounded like he was hacking up his insides.

The doctor had said it was flu, but by Thursday Jack wasn't better—he was worse. So they ran some tests. The chest X-ray showed he had pneumonia. Thursday night, they admitted him to Marshall Memorial Hospital.

Dad drove Logan and me to see him right after school on Friday. I was expecting to see Jack lounging in bed, watching TV, and ordering nurses to bring him strawberry milkshakes and sports magazines. Instead, he lay quietly, hooked up to a bunch of tubes.

Joey and Alice were already there. I took one look at Joey's chalk-colored face and knew that something was majorly wrong.

"Rob," said Alice, as soon as we walked into the room. She seemed calm, except for her left thumb, which was moving rapidly back and forth across her index finger. I'm pretty sure she didn't even know she was doing it.

"They've gotten the results back from the blood test," she said. "Jack has psittacosis."

He has *what?* I thought.

"What is psitta—what did you say?" asked Dad.

"—cosis."

"Psittacosis," he repeated.

"It's an infectious disease," she explained. "From bacteria." She paused. "You get it from parrots."

Alice kept on talking, explaining more stuff, but I didn't hear a word. So many prickly sensations rushed through my body that I thought I'd been injected with a barrel of needles.

Parrots! Jack had *sitta* what? *Sitta*-something-awful. Some weird, horrible, unpronounceable bird disease. And he got it from Elvis! The bird *I* gave him! The stupid, crazy bird I'd been so excited to own so I could trick Dad and Alice into getting me a dog. The GAD plan. The one that killed Tiggy. And now Jack . . .

I wanted to die.

My eyes darted around the room and found Logan's. He looked like he wanted to die, too.

"Dad, Alice," I blurted. "We need to tell you something."

Jack's hand shot out, thumb down, from under his sheet. Logan fired me a look that said, *Shut up, Iz.*

"Not now, honey," said Dad.

Not now, I thought, slumping. Not now, or not ever? I wondered.

On the way home from the hospital, we stopped at the vet's to get tetracycline for Elvis. Then we went to the drugstore to pick up antibiotics for the rest of us. Alice told us the doctor said we could all get sitta-whatever, especially me, from airborne spores in the bird-doo.

When we got home, I went straight to my room, quietly closed my door, and sat down on my bed. I stared at Nelson. He stared at me. Ashamed, I lowered my head. A piece of paper peeked from under the bed. In a daze, I reached for the small white square. It was a vocabulary-word-of-the-day I'd pitched. The word jeered at me.

Prudence: wise thought before acting; good judgment.

I cried.

The guilt I'd felt when Tiggy died was nothing compared to this. Zero. Not anything. This guilt swallowed me whole. It was like drowning in the dark, slimy, stinking belly of a whale.

How serious was *sitta-whatever?* I was afraid to ask. Could Jack die? Could I? Geez, not only was that stuff airborne, it had been cooked on my lightbulb!

Logan tapped on my door, then entered, followed by Joey.

"We looked psittacosis up on the Web," said Logan, gloomily.

Joey looked scared.

"And?" I whispered, wiping away tears with the back of my hand.

Joey's voice quivered. "You can die from it," he said.

A wave of nausea washed over me.

"No, Joey," said Logan. "Only if you're really old." But he didn't sound convinced.

At the Hospital

Maybe I slept some, but I doubt it. Finally, the first rays of sun lightened my curtains. I saw Nelson, silhouetted against the fabric, stalking a fly. He seemed bigger. Had he grown?

I jumped out of bed and pulled on shorts and an almost-clean T-shirt. On my way downstairs, I heard throw-up sounds from Dad's bathroom. Alice? Was she sick now, too? Had Jack thrown up? What were the first symptoms?

I sure as heck didn't know. I hadn't even lived here last week.

Dad was in the kitchen, cooking bacon.

I loved the smell of sizzling bacon—and the sound. But today, both seemed disgusting. How could Dad go about his normal Saturday, like nothing else was going on?

"When do we leave for the hospital?" I asked.

Dad turned to me. "Do you want to go?" He sounded surprised.

"Of course I want to go."

"After we eat," he answered, turning back to flip the bacon.

"Is Alice sick?" I asked.

"Alice?" Dad hesitated. "Sick? Well, no. I mean, yes. A little."

He whirled around when he realized what I must have been thinking. "Not *that* sick," he assured me. "Not psittacosis. She's just feeling a little puny today."

I stared at Dad, scared. He had never been a good liar.

We spent the day at the hospital. All of us. Alice, Dad, Logan, Joey, and me. When Jack was awake, we hovered around him in a circle, smiling, cheering him up. Joey and I perched on the radiator under the window. Dad and Logan leaned against the wall, while Alice sat in the only chair. Everything smelled like Lysol.

When Jack drifted off to sleep, we slouched around in the waiting room. Alice and Dad read magazines. The rest of us wallowed silently in waves of guilt.

Alice, as far as I know, didn't throw up anymore. She looked fine. The teacher side of her popped up once.

"You could all be catching up on your homework," she said.

We ignored her.

By afternoon, even Jack looked better. He wanted one of his survival books to read, so Dad went home to get it.

Dad returned with *My Side of the Mountain*, his favorite. A minute later, Mom showed up, dressed in her tennis clothes.

Mom! I had completely forgotten. We were supposed to play tennis today.

"Alice," she said nervously, stepping inside

Jack's small room that was about as full of people as a hospital room can get. "I'm so sorry about Jack."

Alice returned a warm, we're-both-moms smile.

"How do you feel?" Mom asked Jack, with real concern.

"Okay." Jack smiled, then coughed like crazy.

"Iz." Mom turned to me. "I'm really sorry to barge in. I was so worried when I came to pick you up and no one was home. And no one answered the phone. So later, I drove by again, and ran into Rob."

I could tell she was uncomfortable around all of us—especially Dad. They almost always tried to act polite in front of me, but there were still weird vibes, like the air was painful.

"Your Dad told me you could use a break," she said. "Would you like to come home with me?"

Was she nuts? Was Dad insane? Didn't anybody understand anything?

"No!" I shouted, too loud.

Everyone in the tiny room stared at me.

"I can't leave," I said more quietly, but firmly. "It's my fault Jack's here."

142

"Don't be silly," said Mom. "How can Jack's pneumonia—"

"Iz, don't," said Logan under his breath.

Alice dismissed my confession with a wave of her hand. "Oh, Iz," she said. "Just because he got sick from Elvis, it certainly isn't your—"

"It *is* my fault!" I practically shouted. "It's all our faults. Me, Logan, Joey, Jack. You don't know what we did."

Logan groaned.

Jack closed his eyes, and slid farther under the covers.

"We're toast," said Joey.

I knew my face was sprouting so many red blobs that I probably looked like one of Dad's pepper plants, but I didn't care.

"GAD," I said. "Get-a-Dog. It was our master plan—guaranteed to be so annoying that you and Dad would let us have a dog."

"What?" said Dad, tilting his head, bewildered.

Alice's face went completely blank.

They didn't get it. So I explained everything. The whole stupid, totally botched, plan.

"And then Tiggy died," I ended, lowering my head. "And now Jack . . ." I could feel my eyes filling up with tears, and my voice getting shaky, so I shut up.

For about two seconds, no one said a word. Then everyone talked at the same time. Which, in a room the size of two closets, was wild.

Dad, disappointed: "How could you all be so irresponsible?"

Alice, surprised: "Jack's not going to die. Didn't you hear what I said yesterday?"

Mom, sad: "Oh, Elizabeth, sweetie."

Jack, annoyed: "I can't believe you ratted."

Joey, staggered: "Jack's not going to die?"

Logan, miserable: "It was a lame idea, really lame."

Dad: "No kidding."

Joey: "Will we be punished?"

Jack: "Will I have to get rid of Elvis?"

Dad: "Yes."

Alice: "No."

Dad and Alice: "Maybe."

Jack, sarcastically: "Way to go, Iz."

Everybody's words got shuffled—like a deck of cards—and came out: *How could you die, sweetie? Believe Jack. No lame Elvis. Yes—no—way to go.*

Only one sentence came out clear in my head: "Jack's not going to die."

If Alice had explained that yesterday, I'd definitely missed it.

"Quiet!" commanded Dad.

In the silence that followed, I asked, softly, "Is Jack really going to be okay?"

"Of course," said Alice. "I told you yesterday. Psittacosis *can* be fatal, but that's only likely in infants or someone elderly. Jack's going to be fine." She smiled, leaned forward, and ruffled his hair. "Aren't you, Jack?"

"Heck, yeah," he said. "I'm going to play baseball Monday."

"No, you're not," said Dad sympathetically. "I'm afraid Dr. Shelton says you're out for the season, buddy."

"What? No way!" shouted Jack, right before he doubled over in a coughing fit.

145

Logan, Joey, and I ignored the coughing, and collapsed on him in one big group hug.

"Get off me, you jerks," he wheezed, but he was laughing, too.

We fell away, happy, forgetting just how much trouble we were in.

Dad slipped his arm around Alice's shoulders. They were both shaking their heads at our hopeless stupidity, but I could tell they were proud of all the love that was gushing around. They smiled in spite of themselves.

Joey looked up innocently at their grinning faces and asked, "Does this mean we can get a dog?"

"Not in your lifetime," said Dad.

Jack coughed a few more times. "I *am* going to play ball," he mumbled.

We all grinned at him, and at each other. In fact, we smiled goofily at everyone in the room. Except Mom. Where was Mom?

Mom had split.

Not Fair

Sunday afternoon, Dr. Shelton let Jack come home from the hospital. He would still need to hang out in bed for a week, but overall, he was back to his tough-guy self.

I had called Mom about a million times. Nobody home. Was she really not there, or just not answering my calls? When, I wondered, had she left Jack's hospital room? Before or after the love fest that didn't include her?

So far, Dad and Alice weren't discussing our doofus GAD plan. I guess they were waiting until Jack got home so they could kill us all at the same time. Meanwhile, Logan released his snake back where he'd found him, and Joey let his cricket go.

Then, all three of us set our praying mantises free in Dad's garden.

It just about killed me to say good-bye to Nelson. He was the best listener I'd ever had. But to be honest, he had become way too hard to feed. He wouldn't settle for the dead stuff anymore, and keeping him in live spiders and flies was about to become a full-time job.

So I placed him gently on a tomato seedling, and wished him well. He had pounced on three ants and an aphid before I could turn around. Just knowing that I'd sent Nelson to praying mantis heaven made me feel the best I'd felt in over a week. Then, remembering that I'd helped send Tiggy to hedgehog heaven made me feel awful again.

Our crazy animal house sure had fewer animals than a week ago.

I sighed. As long as my house had Logan, Jack, and Joey living in it, it would always be an animal house. Animal house and Iz. I grinned. How could I not love it?

So where did that leave Mom? I kicked a dirt

clump, waved a good-bye kiss at Nelson, and went inside to call her again.

Still no answer.

After Jack came home and got settled, Dad and Alice called for a family meeting. None of us had a clue what to expect. Would they be happy that Jack was well, and that we'd released our GAD project back into the wild? Or would they ground us for months for trying to trick them?

We met in the den, with Jack stretched out on the sofa, covered in a fleece throw.

Dad and Alice hit us with a lot of what-were-you-thinking questions.

We responded with a lot of I-dunno-but-we're-incredibly-sorry answers.

That seemed to please them.

"So we're not in trouble?" asked Joey.

"Of course you're in trouble," said Dad. "But because of your great attitudes, we're going to let you live here, and we'll still feed you, and maybe send you to college."

Dad could be such a riot sometimes.

"Oh," said Joey.

"You're all grounded," Dad said. "For two weeks."

We shot semi-distressed glances at each other, but as far as I was concerned, being grounded for two weeks was fine. I had a huge lump of guilt that I needed to get rid of.

"Not fair," said Joey. "Jack's got to stay in bed for at least a week anyway."

Jack grinned.

"Does that mean Iz can't go to her Mom's?" asked Logan.

Dad slumped and shot Alice an I'm-tired-you-handle-this-one look.

"Of course Iz can go to her Mom's," said Alice. "That's her home. Well, one of them. As for Jack, he's spent three days in the hospital and is going to miss the rest of baseball season. That's punishment enough."

"It's still not fair," mumbled Joey.

"Life's not fair," answered Alice.

I was pretty sure that *life's not fair* was the

number-one recommended response in every parent and teacher manual on the planet. I bet they instructed you how to say it in Japanese, Swedish, Swahili, and a million other languages I've never even heard of.

Anyway, all four of us, even Joey, knew it wasn't a good time to ask for a dog.

That night, I lay awake missing Nelson and Tiggy, but I was happy that GAD was over, and especially that Jack was home. I touched the orange plastic container of antibiotics on my bedside table, and prayed it would keep me free of sitta-co-something-or-other.

I also thought about Mom—and about what Claire had said. Sure, Claire and her amateur psychiatry phase got carried away a lot—like calling Jack a psychopath—but sometimes she hit close to the truth. *Had* living alone changed Mom? And did fixing that have to be my job?

Heck, even if she turned into Mom of the Year, I'd still want to live with my big, nutty family. Was that so terrible?

But, what worried me the most was—where

was she? Had she gone back to London? Was she lying helpless on her oriental rug with her legs partly nibbled off? Did she hate me, or did she love me?

Monday, I still didn't have a clue how Mom felt, but thirteen losing Warthogs definitely hated me. I guess word had leaked that their star pitcher was toast, mostly on account of me.

Nobody blamed Elvis. Not even Dad and Alice. They said that as soon as the tetracycline cured him, he was Jack's, for better or worse. Fortunately, Jack loved his worst. I couldn't even like his *best*.

After school, Claire came over. She said she wanted to see Jack. Ha!

But, believe it or not, she did go straight upstairs to visit him. She even brought him a strawberry pie that she and her mother had made on Sunday. When Logan came in, she smiled warmly, and said, "Hey, Logan."

Claire's *hey* had only one syllable, not her usual

twelve. Was it just my imagination, or had she been slightly less dorky around Logan lately? Maybe her stupid-flirt routine had been because she was nervous. Now that Logan liked her, would she be regular Claire again?

Who knew? But I was thrilled that I might get out of telling her she made me want to throw up. I was just too tired. And I still had Mom to deal with.

"Iz," Joey called in a nervous voice. "Phone."

Please let it be Mom, I whispered to myself as I hurried down the hall.

Joey handed me the receiver. "It's your mom," he whispered. He looked at me anxiously. He started to say more, but changed his mind.

Suddenly, I panicked. Why did Joey look so weird? Was Mom hurt? Angry? Dying?

I swallowed hard, gripped the receiver like I was shaking hands with Arnold Schwarzenegger, and said hello.

"Iz!" said Mom excitedly. "Finally! I'm so glad

I got you. How's Jack? Can you come over? I've got something to show you." She laughed out loud. "You won't believe it!"

My heart sank. She wasn't dying, hurt, *or* angry. She was *in denial* again.

"Jack's fine," I said.

"I'm so glad." She said it as though she really meant it. "Can you come now? Can you stay for dinner?"

Mom was bubbling over like an uncorked champagne bottle. Was being in denial better than being wounded?

I'd have to think about it.

"I know Alice has her hands full looking after Jack. I'll pick you up. Okay?"

"Sure, Mom," I said. "That'll be fine."

Mom lives ten minutes away. I swear, she got here in five.

The second I slid into the car, I explained, "Mom, I tried and tried to call you."

"I know," she said. "I got your messages. Didn't

Joey tell you I called? Or was it Jack? I've been so busy. Wait till you see—"

Joey. The cute little creep. What had he been reading this time? Or drawing? I made a mental note: Always remember to ask Joey if you've got messages.

"—so not like me. Just wait—" Mom was still bubbling. I couldn't remember when I'd seen her so excited. Maybe back before her job sent her all over the planet. What had excited her then— besides wicked-witch imitations? I smiled. She used to throw fancy dinner parties for Dad and their friends. She had loved doing that.

Planning elegant menus of stuff that took all day to cook. Creating amazing arrangements of exotic flowers. Picking the perfect CD for background music. All those things used to get Mom this excited.

Was she planning an elegant party for all her friends? Did she still have friends, or had she been away too much? I didn't even know.

When we got to her townhouse, Mom practically sprinted up the steps. She flung open her door and scurried to the kitchen.

"Wait here," she called back to me. "Close your eyes."

Somehow, I didn't like the feel of this. What had she done?

Mom's Surprise

"Are your eyes closed?" asked Mom, peeking her head around the kitchen door and grinning.

"Yes, Mom."

I squeezed my eyes shut.

"Okay, sweetheart. Open them."

I opened my eyes. It took me half a second to focus. Oh my God! What was that?! It couldn't be! But it was.

Mom stood proudly by the kitchen door, holding it open. By her feet sat the ugliest dog I'd ever seen in my entire life. Part of me was furious. I couldn't believe she was still trying to bribe me with a dog! Another part of me wanted to laugh hysterically at the creature sitting by her feet.

157

How could anyone be bribed with *that* dog?

She looked kind of like a bulldog. Same short, bent legs and smushed face. But she was a stick-figure bulldog, something Joey would have drawn when he was four years old. Skinny. Not unhealthy or starved, though. No. This dog was built thin.

Her eyes locked on mine and clearly said, *love me.* I didn't know whether to laugh or hug her.

Instead, I yelled at Mom.

"Mom!" I shouted. "How could you?"

"How could I what?" said Mom, baffled.

"Keep trying to win me over with stupid stuff!"

Mom's face went through about a million frames per second. Surprise, confusion, recognition, horror.

"Oh, Iz!" she exclaimed. "No. This dog isn't for you. This dog is for me." She paused and thought for a second. "Okay, maybe I did try to bribe you before. But not this time." She gazed lovingly at mystery mutt, scooped her up, and kissed her, smack on her caved-in nose.

158

"And this little sunshine is not stupid!" she added defensively.

I thought *I* was her sunshine.

Mom set the dog back on the floor, walked quickly toward me, and folded me into a warm hug. Then she held me back at arm's length, and said, "Iz, let's sit down. I have so much to tell you."

We walked into the living room. Mom sat on one side of the sofa. I sat on the other. Ugly mutt sat on the floor between us and looked eagerly back and forth.

Mom made her hands into a steeple in front of her face. She thought a moment, then lowered them.

"I love you," she said, looking directly into my eyes. "But I understand why you can't move in with me." She hesitated. "In Jack's room at the hospital—"

"Oh, Mom," I interrupted. "I looked for you. When did you leave? We didn't mean to—"

"Iz," said Mom, softly. "Shhh. It's all right. What I saw told me everything you've been try-ing to tell me, and I wouldn't listen. You have

159

a family that loves you, and you love them, and . . ." Her voice was suddenly quivery, so she stopped.

"It's okay," she said, quietly. Then she laughed. A real, from-the-heart, genuine laugh. "I'd go bonkers in less than two minutes if I lived with that crew. But, it *is* you." She corrected herself. "It is Iz."

"Oh, Mom." I wanted to cry. Instead, I reached down and picked up ugly-dog, because she was leaning against my leg, saying, *excuse me, I'm here.*

"Uh, Mom," I said, stroking one soft, saggy ear. "This is not a bichon."

"No kidding," said Mom, brightening. "That's the other thing I wanted to tell you. When I left the hospital, I can't tell you how alone I felt."

"Mom," I protested.

"No." She put out her arm as though holding me off. "Let me finish. I went straight to the farmer's market. You know nothing cheers me up like fresh ingredients. I planned to pick out the best lettuces, the most exotic vegetables, and take them home and create a salad that could be on the cover of *Gourmet* magazine."

She paused and smiled, not at me, but at the dog whose ear I was scratching.

"They were hosting an Adopt-A-Pet event outside the market. Dozens of owners were there with pets that needed homes. I walked right by them, of course. What a yapping, whining mixture of mutts. And then I saw her." She gazed tenderly at . . .

"Mom," I asked, "what *is* her name?"

"Cleopatra," she said.

"Cleopatra!" I practically choked.

Mom laughed. "I know she's not beautiful, but there is something irresistible about her. Her eyes, I think. Besides, you know I love Shakespeare— and *Antony and Cleopatra* is my favorite play. I knew I wanted her before I learned what her name was, but that clinched it."

Mom wiggled her eyebrows up and down, and did a silly, spooky music imitation that reminded me of her wicked-witch routine. "I think Cleopatra and I are destined," she said. Then she clapped her hands together. "The best part is that she's grown, so she's already housebroken, and she won't chew on my carpets."

Suddenly, Mom sagged a little. She looked questioningly at me, then added, "I suppose you'll want to call her Cleo."

I cupped Cleopatra's smashed-in face in my hands. She was so ugly, she was almost cute. "I don't know, Mom. Cleopatra's fine." I hesitated. "She's just so . . . so . . ."

"Not *me*," said Mom.

"Well, yeah," I said. "Not you."

Mom picked a strand of dog hair off her slacks, and sighed. "It struck me on my last trip to London that I've been, well, missing out on something. Not just needing to see more of you, but, I don't know, something else. Something crazy. Does that make sense?"

"Yeah, Mom." My heart did a warm, electric flip-flop. I smiled. "That makes lots of sense."

"And Cleopatra is the craziest thing I've ever seen. But she's quality crazy, you know? Not pedigreed, of course, but real. And for some reason, which I will never be able to explain, I had to bring her home."

I looked into Cleopatra's warm, dancing eyes. They pulled me in and touched me, tingly and deep.

Mom grinned and threw up her hands. "But we've barely been home at all. First thing, I had to get her checked at the vet. Then we took a walk. Next, I had to show her off to some of my old friends. . . ."

I slid over closer to Mom and gave her a bear hug, sandwiching Cleopatra snugly between us. She stretched her tongue straight up, trying to lick both our faces.

"And one more thing," said Mom, wiping her chin. "I had no idea that you and your . . . brothers wanted a dog *that* badly. I know you said that Rob and Alice didn't want a pet that could mess up their vacation plans, but I have an idea."

So far, Mom had been a barrel of surprises. What next?

"Maybe," she said, "I could help out on occasional weekends. You know—keep an extra dog for a couple of days, if you think it would help."

Mom looked at me expectantly. Was this really my mom?

"Of course, it couldn't be a Great Dane or anything, and it would have to be well mannered . . . and housebroken."

Yep. It was my mom.

Animal House and *What?*

It felt weird when Mom dropped me back home. Alice was right when she'd said I have two homes. And suddenly, spending more time at Mom's didn't seem so awful anymore. Not because of Cleopatra and a bunch of tropical fish, either. Because of Mom.

And because of me. Finally, I understood her— especially the *missing out* part.

Even stranger—the whole thing made me feel better about Claire. If Mom could accept sharing me with Dad, I bet I could get the hang of sharing Claire with Logan. Especially if regular Claire came back.

I waved a kiss good-bye to Mom and Cleopatra, and flew up our front steps. I couldn't wait

165

to tell Logan, Jack, and Joey that Mom would baby-sit a dog for us—if only we could convince Dad and Alice to get one. After GAD, I doubted there'd be much chance of that, but at least it would make it a lot easier for me to tell them that I had a dog now, and they didn't.

Why is it, when one lump of guilt starts to go away, another one slips right in and takes its place?

"I'm home!" I shouted, letting the front door slam in my hurry to find my brothers.

I could hear Dad and Alice washing dishes and putting away pots and pans in the kitchen. I wondered what they'd eaten for dinner. Geez. How long would it take me to stop worrying about everything I missed?

As I headed upstairs, I heard Alice asking Dad, "Don't you think we should let the kids pick a name?"

I stopped, frozen in mid-step. What! A name? A name for what? Yes! It had to be. I couldn't believe it. We were getting a dog!

I tore up the steps, leaping two at a time.

"Logan, Jack, Joey!" I yelled, running down the hall.

I flew into Jack and Joey's room. All three of them were sprawled across the beds, watching the TV that Dad had moved there for Jack.

"Guess what!" I said, gulping for breath. "I just heard Alice. We're getting a dog. She said we could name it!"

"What?"

"No!"

"You're kidding, right?"

"No, I'm not kidding." I repeated exactly what I'd heard, and then I told them all about Mom and Cleopatra, and how she'd even offered to keep our dog sometimes.

"Yippee!" shouted Joey.

"Yea!" Jack exclaimed, without coughing once.

"Awesome," whispered Logan, sliding off Joey's bed and sitting on the floor.

"*Squaaawk!*" Even Elvis was excited. Either that, or he needed to poop.

"But, listen," I warned. "We've got to sound surprised when they tell us."

"Easy," said Joey, grinning from ear to ear.

"Sure," said Logan, with one elbow propped up on the mattress. "Do you think your mom called mine and told her she'd dog-sit? Why else would they change their minds?"

"I don't know," I answered. "Maybe they felt sorry for us because we wanted a dog so bad we turned dumb and dumber. Maybe Mom did call them, but I doubt it. I think she would have told me."

"Unless they're planning the surprise together," said Joey.

I tried to imagine Mom and Alice plotting. Not Dad and Mom. No way. But Mom and Alice? Maybe.

"Iz," Alice called up the steps. "Is that you?"

"Yeah!" I yelled back.

"Could you guys come downstairs for a minute?"

"Be right there!" I shouted.

We all just about split our faces grinning at each other.

"Stay cool," Logan whispered, as we strolled casually into the den.

"Rob and I have a surprise for you," said Alice, the second we all sat down.

I gave my full attention to Alice. I knew if I looked at Logan, Jack, or Joey, I'd lose it.

Alice grinned at Dad. Dad grinned at Alice.

"Yeah?" said Logan, trying to sound relaxed and totally uninterested. "What's up?"

"You tell them," said Alice.

"No, you, honey," said Dad.

"Somebody tell us!" screamed Jack.

Uh, oh, I thought. Jack and Joey will never pull this off if Dad and Alice don't hurry up.

"Well," said Alice slowly, "we think you're going to love our news."

Dad winked at Alice.

"We're going to have a brand-new addition to the Becker household."

"Yes!" shouted Joey. "A dog! Can I name it?"

Alice and Dad looked at each other, startled.

I wanted to strangle Joey. He was ruining their surprise.

"No," said Alice, thrown off slightly, but smiling again. "Not a dog."

Not a dog! Did she say, *not a dog?*

Alice reached over and squeezed Dad's hand. "We're having a baby," she said.

A what? A baby?!

The silence was numbing. No one said a word.

My insides were flipping through emotions faster than my brain could log them in. No dog— terrible. A baby—fantastic. Wait. Dad and Alice's baby? Confusion. Weren't they too old for that? Embarrassment. Apparently not. Whoa! I'm going to have another brother. Cool . . . maybe. No. Yes. Or a sister! Definitely yes. Incredible!

I jumped up to hug Alice, then Dad.

He squeezed me extra tight and whispered, "my Little Iz Whiz."

"A baby," said Logan, grinning sheepishly. "Awesome. I think."

"Yes!" exclaimed Jack. "I won't be the youngest." Then he frowned. "I'm not sharing my room with any more people."

"Can I baby-sit?" asked Joey.

Dad and Alice laughed.

"One question at a time," said Dad.

But that didn't happen. We all kept asking questions, one on top of the other. And Dad and Alice did their best to answer them.

When?

December.

A new house?

Maybe—or build an addition to this one.

A pink nursery or a blue one?

Don't know—yet.

How about black?

Get serious, Jack.

Names?

Who knows? What do you guys think?

Emily, Russell, Jen, Eric, Hannah, Andy, Kate, Hagrid, Jabba-the-Hut, Cookie Monster, Shiloh.

As the excitement died down a little, I was bursting to tell them about Cleopatra, and that Mom would baby-sit a dog for us, but *duh*. I knew

171

that would have to wait. Clearly, the timing was wrong.

"Iz's mom said we could get a dog!" blurted Joey.

I groaned, then gave damage control my best shot—again.

I explained everything.

Dad looked majorly skeptical. "Your mom said that? And she brought home an ugly dog?"

"Yeah, Dad. Weird, huh? She's tired of missing out."

"Your mom?" he repeated, faintly.

"How thoughtful," said Alice.

They didn't say yes. But they didn't say no, either.

Like I said. It was bad timing. They were way too wrapped up in glowing and planning ahead to give much thought to a dog.

No kidding. Dad and Alice were planning ahead!

And there were going to be seven of us!

I laughed out loud. Animal House, Iz, and a baby! It sounded just like a movie.

I couldn't wait to be in it.